WIDE AS THE
Wind

Edward Stanton

Open Books Press
Bloomington, Indiana

Copyright © 2016 Edward Stanton

All rights reserved. No part of this book may be reproduced or
transmitted in any form or by any means, electronic or mechanical,
including photocopying, recording, or by any information storage and
retrieval system, without permission in writing from the publisher.

Published by Open Books Press, USA

www.OpenBooksPress.com
info@OpenBooksPress.com

An imprint of Pen & Publish, Inc.
www.PenandPublish.com
Bloomington, Indiana
(314) 827-6567

Print ISBN: 978-1-941799-38-3
eBook ISBN: 978-1-941799-39-0

Library of Congress Control Number: 2016908616

Sooty Tern image by Richard Crossley via Wikimedia Commons

Author photo: Benita Clarke

for Melissa

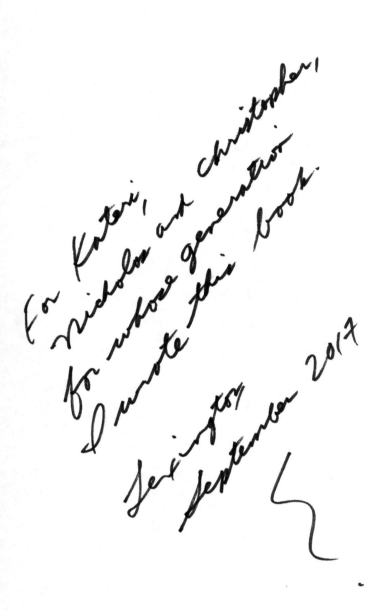

For Katari,
Nicholas and Christopher,
for whose generation
I wrote this book.

Lexington
September 2017

Aûé ê nua ê, aûé ê koro ê, aûé nga kope ê

O my mother, O my father, O my people

Contents

Chapter 1

Call

Dawn spread white wings across the sky. Miru awoke, aware that it was the day when he must travel to the forbidden grove. Outside a rooster crowed. As he imagined the priestess in her dank cave, the boy shivered. He strapped a knife of obsidian to one arm.

He walked on bare feet over the earthen floor. Miru saw his mother by the hearth, where last night's embers glowed. He ran to her. Smiling, Ia pressed her nose against her son's. With the long fingers of one hand she grazed the freckles on his cheeks.

"Good morning," she said with her voice like water. Miru's features had come from her: he had his mother's brown skin, her dark hair and green eyes the color of the sea.

From the fire Ia pulled a yam. She set it on a wooden plate to cool. With sleepy eyes Miru stared at it, feeling a pang of hunger. He knew that she had roasted the yam for his father. As soon as his mother turned away, Miru snatched it and scurried out the door.

He squatted on the ground by the family's well. Using his knife, he cut through the warm yam's skin as he had seen fishermen slit a mackerel's belly. Steam rose from the yellow pulp and filled the child's nostrils.

As Miru ate with his fingers, he watched the life that stirred around him in the square: dogs rousing from sleep, pigs rooting in the dust, birds hopping, roosters, hens and their chicks pecking the dirt. Curls of smoke seeped through the thatch walls of houses. When a fly landed on Miru's foot, he kicked. It flew away. As he always did when he was happy, he wiggled his toes, smiling.

He yearned to be with his mother at the hearth again. But he knew she would scold him for eating his father's food. Miru also remembered that he must journey to the seer's grotto today. Why would the old sorceress want me to go there, he wondered.

The boy could not resist peeking through the door. He spotted his mother by the hearth. Without looking at her son she asked, "Why did you steal your father's food?" Even when she tried to be stern, Ia's voice sounded like coursing water.

"I was so hungry, Mother." The child entered.

"I cooked taro for you."

"I'm tired of taro," he said, drawing closer. "We all used to eat yams— why can't I eat them now?"

Ia placed her thin hands on Miru's shoulders. Already the boy knew she would not scold him. "The enemy has burned many of our fields. The harvest of yams is reserved for soldiers who need strength to fight, like your father."

"I need strength too—I'm going to make a long trip today."

She pulled the boy to her side. Miru buried his face in his mother's belt of tapa cloth. "You've already eaten the yam, right?"

"Yes."

"Then go before your father wakes. Be careful, my son." She rubbed the braids of his dark-brown hair. Passing one hand over his brow, she gave Miru her blessing.

He spun and rushed over the threshold. In the square he scattered the chickens, birds, pigs and dogs. Miru ran through sparse woods to the coast. With his braids swinging behind him, he dashed along the beach, splashing in small waves. He felt a light and foamy ease until the witch's cave returned to his mind.

Miru stopped at the cove where he and Kenetéa often met in secret. On the sand he recognized her shapely footprints. He would have liked to wait for her there instead of going to the cavern—show her his tattoos, the new markings on his face, chest and shoulders. But Miru continued on his way, staying clear of fields where armies were already skirmishing in the early light. He could hear the cries of soldiers and the clashing of weapons.

Day moved across the world. Before noon he had entered the secluded grove, the thickest forest on Vaitéa. Miru shuddered as he tiptoed through the shady woods. When he approached the cave, a guard challenged him, raising his lance.

"The priestess called me here," Miru said. "I'm Koro's son." Hearing that warrior's name, the man bowed his head, lowered his spear and led the visitor to the cavern's mouth.

Miru crawled into the blackness. When he stood up, he bumped his head on the stony ceiling. Slowly his eyes grew accustomed to the dark. Keeping low, he moved forward, groping with both hands along moist walls. Miru came to a large chamber where he could stand without stooping. He smelled a musty odor, old as the world. Waves crashed on the rocks below.

"Welcome to my sanctuary, Miru!" a voice boomed from the grotto's depths. The boy looked around him: he could see nobody.

"I'm here!" the voice called, behind him now, laughing, echoing against the walls. He whirled. He still could not see the sorceress.

A torch flared ahead of him, and a woman appeared in a circle of light. Swaying from side to side, her body covered in a cape of bark-cloth, her head topped by a tall cone of feathers, Marama moved toward him. As she walked, Miru heard the rustling of her garment and the creaking of her bones.

She extinguished the torch and dropped it on the cave floor. Marama rubbed the boy's chest where it was tattooed with a pair of leaping dolphins. "The artist captured your spirit-animals well," she told him. He did not understand how the woman could see in the darkness. But after all, he thought, Marama had been named for the moon.

With her hand she brushed his shoulders and their images of breaking waves. Finally Marama skimmed the lines that the tattooer had etched on Miru's face with birdbone needles. "You are beginning to resemble a man," she said.

Without warning the seer grasped his arm with one hand. Her sharp fingernails, curved like a bird's talons, broke Miru's skin. For the first time in his young life he felt fear in his chest.

"Look at this eye," Marama told him, pointing to her good one, the left, with her free hand. Miru was becoming used to the dark, but he could scarcely discern that eye. "It sees the world," she said. Marama touched her other eye, the right, blank as the moon. "See this one? It's blind yet it perceives more and greater things—those that are invisible to you and others." Water dripped from the cavern walls. "So listen to what will change your life forever, Miru."

The witch paused to draw a breath. "Our people think we suffer because the tribes are at war, because we're ruled by men with bloody hands. They're wrong. It's something larger than all of us."

"What?" Miru's voice echoed in the chamber.

"Our land and our seas are dying," Marama intoned. "We've razed our forests and poisoned our shores so that our nesting birds, our fish and shellfish have dwindled or disappeared. Fighting has despoiled our land. Many people are hungry. Your own mother cooks less food for your family."

"How did you know?"

"I know many things, sometimes before they happen." Marama tightened her grip on the boy's left arm. "You must sail to an island far away, Miru, to bring back the seeds and shoots of new trees, to restore our woods and rescue Vaitéa."

"What!" His eyes looked big as oysters. "We live at the end of the world! Nobody has ever reached another island—how could I?" Miru remembered Kenetéa.

"You must forget her."

He failed to comprehend how the priestess could steal his thoughts. Recalling the girl's skin, smooth as mother-of-pearl, he said, "I cannot forget."

"Her tribe is locked in war with ours." Marama allowed her utterance to sink into Miru's mind. "Anyway you'll never love her or any other woman until you pass the rite and leave this cave as a man."

Those words ran through him like a spear. Trying to hold back the tears welling in his eyes, he drooped his head. "Marama," he said, "my father has trained me to be a soldier so I can defend our family and our tribe." Without thinking Miru clasped the hilt of his dagger with his right hand.

"Your father's a great soldier but your mission is more crucial than war. You're the last boy who's been schooled as a sailor, right?"

"Yes."

"Your family owns the best longboat on Vaitéa, true?"

Miru nodded. "But it takes a crew of three to sail it," he said. "All our men are at war or have died in battle."

"You'll have to find a crew."

He did not reply. It was useless to argue with Marama, who had an answer for everything. A roller smashed on the shore with a sound like a huge tree cracking. He thought of bright-eyed Kenetéa.

The priestess loosened her hold on Miru's arm. "Listen to me," she said softly, leaning forward. He could smell her odor of smoke and ashes. "The time has come, Miru. You must sacrifice your love for Kenetéa in order to save our island home." She pressed the boy's arm with both hands.

He was trapped in the grotto, sickened by Marama's clammy touch, her nails and the stench of her body. He no longer felt afraid. Miru pushed the seer's hands away.

Marama knew the sadness of an old woman whose body revolts a young man. Yet she drew nearer, so close that he could feel her breath on his face now, smell it. She stroked Miru's chest. Marama raised both arms beneath her cape, swelling in the dark like a bird with wide wings.

"Son of Koro," she said in her sonorous voice, "at your birth-feast I predicted you would be headstrong—"

"Like you, Marama?"

The witch smiled. "Yes. And in you I've almost met my match." She paused. "Few sons are as good as their fathers—in fact most are worse. I thought you might be different. But you're a slave of your own heart."

"No son or father could make that voyage."

"Aayy!" Marama cried in a wail so piercing, so painful that it seemed to shake the roots of the earth. Aiming a crooked finger at the boy's face, she said, "I've never banished anyone from this cave. You're the first, Miru. Go! Don't return until you're brave enough to hear my call."

His face burned with shame. The sorceress, who could see so clearly in the dark, watched Miru's cheeks flush. With both hands he covered his face. Then he stood straight and bumped his head on the ceiling again. As he slunk from the cavern, Marama smiled with cunning.

Chapter 2

Rope of Knowledge

Like an animal Miru skulked through the secret grove, disgraced for being expelled from the sanctuary. Tears glistened on his cheeks. He wandered along the coast, through forests, over fields and hills. Observing the dried grass, the stumps, withered bushes and trees, Miru realized that he had hardly noticed them before.

He heard the rumble of soldiers marching from a distance. Suddenly Miru felt a sharp love for his island, for the people, a keenness like a crab's claws pinching at his heart. He wanted to hold them, his tribe and their enemies, all of them in his arms; they went on with their lives, fighting battles without an inkling of the fate Marama had revealed to him in her grotto. They slaughtered each other while their seas, meadows and woods were dying around them.

In the deepening light he walked over parched fields. Miru reached the square in front of his family's great-house. Renga Roiti stood by the well, watching the sky, her red braids shimmering in the last rays of sun. At her feet a pair of dogs was asleep in the dirt.

"Look out there!" she told Miru. "Can you see them?"

He scanned the horizon. "What?"

"What do you think? My birds!" the girl shouted, pointing toward the sea. Miru strained his eyes: far out on the edge of sight he could detect black spots moving against the darkening horizon. They grew larger, their calls more distinct, louder as they flew closer. Renga Roiti skipped up and down, clapping her hands, unable to contain her joy. Clouding the sky, the flock of sooty terns swept overhead.

"This means spring is near," she told Miru. "They went out to sea at dawn and they're returning to their roosts at dusk. But there are fewer birds than before."

He fixed his eyes on Renga Roiti.

Still gazing at the terns she asked, "Brother, why are you gaping at me?" It was as if she could see him from the corners of her eyes. He said nothing. "Look at them!" the girl screamed.

"I can't, Renghi."

"Why not?"

"Because your birds just shit on my head."

Renga Roiti saw the white droppings that streaked Miru's face and dark-brown hair. She laughed. "That's a sign of good luck!" she cried. "You've been anointed."

"Why don't they hit your head?"

"Because they're my totem sisters." She laughed again.

Miru looked forlorn. He had been banned from Marama's cave, ordered to leave Kenetéa and make a wild voyage into the unknown. Now his head and face were dripping fresh guano.

Seeing her brother so dejected, the girl said, "Come over here, Miru."

He walked to the lip of the well, where she drew water and washed him. When she had finished, Renga Roiti studied him and said, "By the way, you look like a ghost." He smiled for the first time since leaving Marama's cave. Miru could always count on his sister to tell him the truth.

He walked through the door, crossed the kitchen and entered the longroom. Ia and Koro were sitting next to a fire that smoldered in the hearth. Both glanced up at their son. His mother smiled.

Ia rose on the floor of tamped earth to welcome him, rubbing her nose against Miru's. She moved with grace, with the halo of royalty around her. When people saw her pass, they said, "Shining Ia walks like a queen."

"Where did you go?" she asked Miru. Her voice sounded like waves lapping on the shore.

He lowered his eyes as his mother caressed his dark braids. "Don't worry about the yam," she whispered in Miru's ear. "I found another one and cooked it for your father."

Casting a shadow over his wife and son, Koro stood. Dirt from the battlefield coated his face. His eyes were gray like winter fog. His beard and braids had the reddish color of yams.

"Good evening, Miru," he said. Koro's voice made the walls of the room tremble.

The boy struggled to speak. "Father, can you summon the family?"

The soldier had never seen his son so gaunt and troubled. "Yes."

They assembled in the longroom: Miru's mother and father, Ia and Koro; red-haired Renga Roiti; their uncle Ihu, priest of the tribe. All took seats around the hearth.

"I have something to announce," Miru declared in a voice they had not heard before. A fly droned in the room. "Marama has called me to sail to another island, to bring back seeds and shoots and to reforest Vaitéa."

The room was silent. All turned to Koro, who was rising to his feet. The soldier inhaled a slow breath. His chest expanded, showing his tattoos of a breaching orca on one side, a sperm whale spewing water from its blowhole on the other.

Koro looked down at his son. "I've drilled you patiently to be a soldier, Miru. As soon as you pass the final ritual of manhood, you must become a warrior to help me defend our family and our people."

"I'll fight when I come back to Vaitéa," the boy said. His uncle, wise Ihu, smiled at the confidence of youth. Neither he nor anyone knew that Miru's doubts and fears were deep.

"Even if you made the journey," Koro said, "even if you returned—and who has ever done that?—it would be too late. By that time the enemy could vanquish us for good. They already control the kingship and they're poised to attack. Miru, we need soldiers now."

"There are other ways to defend a family and a tribe," Ihu interposed, standing. He was the only man on the island as tall as Koro. "In the long flow of time," the priest said, "this voyage may be more urgent than Miru's presence on the battlefield."

"If he doesn't fight, there won't be a family or tribe," Koro responded. His eyes moistened as he spoke to his son: "Remember that I lost both of my brothers in combat." Those words pierced Miru's chest like a lance. Pointing to the dagger sheathed on his son's arm, the soldier asked, "Do you recall what I told you when I gave you this knife?" The boy hung his head without replying. "That you would thrust that weapon to avenge your uncles' deaths one day. You and I are the last males who can protect our house and our clan."

Miru rose while his uncle sat on the earthen floor. Never before had the boy stood face to face with Koro in the longroom. "I'm sorry—" he started with a quaver in his voice. "I'm sorry that I cannot help you in the wars now. But I've made my decision." Miru's voice grew louder: "I didn't come here to ask for your leave, Father." Koro, that mountain of a man, scraped the floor with one foot. "I came for your permission to let my sister sail with me."

All gasped, staring at Renga Roiti. The girl's eyes appeared bigger than clams. She tried to restrain her delight.

"She's too young to be tattooed or marry," Koro said without bothering to look at his daughter. "Your sister needs a parent's consent to leave the great-house." He paused. "I refuse to give my approval, Miru. Anyway," Koro ended with scorn, "no girl or woman has ever sailed in a longboat."

"Renghi could be the first," Miru replied. The girl rose to her feet. Puffed with pride, her little chest heaved.

Renga Roiti stepped toward Koro. The girl had never dared to approach her father in the longroom; she stood side by side with Miru. Her small body quivered. "I know the flights of seabirds better than anyone," she said. "The terns fly out to sea in the morning to fish and wing homeward at nightfall for rest. In this way my spirit sisters could lead our ship to landfall on another island." The girl exchanged glances with Miru.

"You do not have my consent!" their father shouted.

"Koro," Ia inquired, "do you recall the seer's prophecies at our daughter's birth-feast?" She stood. In her voice like water she told her husband, "Marama predicted that Renga Roiti would aid her brother in his sacrifice for Vaitéa and our people."

Koro paid no attention to those words; he was a soldier and did not care about prophecies. Looking straight at Miru, he asked, "When has a boy of fifteen years made a journey like this?"

"I'll turn sixteen in summer."

Again amusement showed on Ihu's countenance, deepening the wrinkles around his eyes. But tears streaked Ia's face—she stood to lose one child on land if her son stayed to fight, two at sea if both children sailed on a voyage. Her brother Ihu comforted the woman, holding her dark hands. In the corner a fly buzzed. Koro pawed the floor with one foot, then the other.

Ia drew close to Miru and hugged him. "You have my approval to take Renga Roiti on the journey," she said. When his mother spoke those words, the boy's heart warmed.

Rising again, Ihu added solemnly, "You have my consent too."

Koro wheeled and rushed to the armory behind the great-house. He gathered a sword, shield and spear in his arms and strode away, looking like the warrior that he was. When he had gone, it seemed an army had broken camp.

Facing her son again in the longroom, Ia told him, "I beg you to make peace with your father."

Leaning on his staff of precious sandalwood, the priest said, "Miru, your mother's right—Koro's the head of our family and leader of our clan." Ihu paused. "There's something else, my nephew. You've been chosen to lead an expedition that could save our island. Your life is not your own now—it belongs to our people. You can no longer be as wild as a dolphin. You must be careful, Miru."

The boy felt the weight of his quest. Not only must he renounce his love for Kenetéa: he must also give up his freedom and the spirit of his totem brothers, the leaping dolphins.

In the darkness Ia led her children across the square. They squeezed her hand to show their gratitude. Together they approached a house shaped like an upturned canoe: it had ribs of great-palm, the wood once used by shipbuilders to make the masts, hulls and keels of boats in the fleet.

The three crossed the threshold, grooved and deepened by time. It was cooler inside. For a moment Miru felt the calm he had always known in his grandfather's home.

Te Rahai rose to greet his family. Like the rigging of an ancient canoe, his body creaked. He had a brown frame, bent and tautened by years of stepping masts, hoisting sails and plying paddles. The old sailor rubbed noses with his daughter and his two grandchildren.

"Father," Ia told him, "Miru wants to sail on your longboat." Showing teeth yellowed by age and wisdom, Te Rahai exulted. He embraced the boy. "Miru has accepted Marama's call to travel across the seas to another island," Ia ended.

"Why?" the mariner inquired, stepping back with eyes opened wide.

"To harvest seeds and shoots," Miru responded, "to bring them back here and reforest our island."

The sailor observed his grandson with eyes full of sorrow. More than anyone on Vaitéa he knew the dangers of embarking on such a journey, a passage from which nobody had ever returned. But gradually his expression changed as he considered Miru's words. "It's true that I've seen many changes on the island, its coasts and waters," Te Rahai told him. "Perhaps the witch has her reasons."

"There's one more thing," Ia said, placing a hand on her father's arm. "Koro wants Miru to stay and help him fight the other tribe."

The old man thought in silence. "I know your husband, Ia. I understand why he would want his only son at his side. But there are many soldiers in our tribe. There's only one sailor who could lead this crossing—Miru. And there's only one ship for him to sail—my twin-hulled canoe." Te Rahai reflected. "Old Marama could be right. The forests have thinned. There are fewer seabirds, fish and shellfish on our island and our seas. Many people on the coast are hungry."

He turned to his grandson. "Miru, you have my permission to make the voyage in my longboat." In his mind the boy could see that vessel standing in dry dock—its two masts and hulls, its prow taller than a greathouse. "You've already proved your seamanship on the outrigger," the sailor told him. "I'll train you on the large ship." Te Rahai paused. "Who will be the members of your crew?"

Renga Roiti jumped in front of her grandfather. "I'm one!"

Stroking the girl's red braids, Te Rahai smiled. "It's taboo for a girl or woman to sail, little bird. And your brother needs two seasoned oarsmen."

"There's nobody else," Miru said. "The times have changed—we're at war, our island's in danger and the taboos no longer hold. You could teach

Renghi as you taught me." Miru remembered those days, the gladdest of his childhood.

Te Rahai removed his hand from the girl's head. "Even a grown woman doesn't have the strength to crew a longboat," he said.

"What if you sailed with us?" Miru asked.

The sailor's laughter echoed from the walls. "I haven't been to sea for so long—ever since I trained you. I'm too aged and feeble," Te Rahai lamented through his white beard, bleached by years at sea. "And the law of generations forbids me to sail on a vessel whose pilot is my grandson." The man hesitated. "How could you think of making the voyage without securing a full crew?"

Miru blushed. "Marama says I must follow her call in order to pass the final test of manhood." He cast his eyes on the floor of tamped earth.

"What does the hag know about ships?" Te Rahai scoffed. "Marama has knowledge of our land but she's never gotten her toes wet. She's spent most of her life in a stinking cave."

He placed his gnarled hands on Miru's shoulders. "In spite of the dangers, I'll take on the task. Every youth needs an old man to guide him," Te Rahai said, breathing fast. "And every old man needs a youth to teach the rope of knowledge."

The sailor turned to size up Renga Roiti. "I don't know about you, little daughter. What would the old seamen say if they learned I was allowing a girl to sail on my canoe?"

"You could tell them that my totem sister's the sacred tern," she responded firmly. "You could say that I know how to spot seabirds better than any man—they can lead us to another island. And you could tell those sailors that if they're so wise and brave, why don't they come with us?" Te Rahai patted her on the head. "Will you show me how to sail?" Renga Roiti begged. Nothing could daunt her.

"Maybe."

The girl clasped her grandfather's brown legs. "How long would it take?"

"Forever, little bird," Te Rahai laughed. But his countenance looked grave when he spoke to his grandson. "You'd still need a third member of the crew." He paused to think. "We're now at the end of winter. You'd have to sail before mid-spring and the rainy season with its foul weather." He sighed. "If you were lucky—most lucky—you might reach an island where you could wait out the season of summer storms and sail home in the fall."

There was a silence in the room. All realized how long Miru and the girl would be gone if they took the voyage, even if it was successful—how far they would have to journey from Vaitéa. Ia strained to hold back the tears seeping from her eyes. Only Renga Roiti appeared unworried, too young to understand the perils of a quest over unknown seas, the slippery path of death.

Chapter 3

Kenetéa

In the morning Te Rahai led his grandchildren to the harbor. He sat down with them on paving stones that glittered with brine and fish scales, where elderly men talked or dozed in the sun. There he told Miru and Renga Roiti about the days when fleets of canoes had covered the waters, shipping crops, stores and people from one end of the island to the other, crossing the shark-roads in search of teeming shoals of fish. The old man also reminded them that murderers had been set adrift and never returned.

With a knife of obsidian Te Rahai helped his grandchildren whittle a toy boat from toromiro wood. Over the next few days he showed them how to cut full-sized paddles for ships. He instructed them to weave sails of pounded bark, to make nets of mulberry cloth and to fashion birdbone hooks.

Miru was grateful to try those crafts again. They attracted him more than the warrior's skills that Koro had taught him: thrusting a knife, swinging a war club and hurling a great-shafted spear. The boy could not have known that he would need all of a soldier's and a sailor's prowess to confront what lay ahead of him.

At night he dreamt of Koro. Recalling his mother's words, he asked himself if he would ever make peace with his father. Wished-for Kenetéa appeared in many dreams too.

Te Rahai schooled Renga Roiti in his grandson's outrigger canoe. With Miru's assistance he trained the girl to thrust forward with quick strokes of an oar. But she was too weak to propel the boat through breakers to the open sea.

The old mariner showed her how to coast the island, to change tack by shifting the mast, reversing bow and stern. With his white beard blowing in the wind, he taught Renga Roiti to navigate by land, sun, moon and stars. He educated her about winds, currents and constellations. Meanwhile Miru discovered that he had forgotten most of their names.

Te Rahai took his grandchildren to fishing grounds near the shore. By torchlight he trained them to catch eels and crayfish. He showed them how to find the royal reserves in deep bluewater, home of great-sharks, whales and giant tuna.

Their yield was light. "In the old days we would have loaded our canoe to the gunnels," Te Rahai told them. Addressing the girl, he said, "Little bird, even when your brother was your age, our take would fill a small boat."

Miru remembered those times. "There are fewer dolphins too," he said. "I have to swim farther beyond the surf to reach them."

"And fewer birds on the land and sea," Renga Roiti added. "They're vanishing like the fish, shellfish and trees."

Old Marama was right, Miru thought: our island is changing.

When the dolphins swam and leaped at the ship's bow, he asked Te Rahai to drop sail. The boy dove into the sea, swam hard, sounded and surfaced where his totem brothers were roiling the water. He played with the dolphins until the old man steered close in the outrigger, handed the helm to Renga Roiti, extended one arm and pulled his grandson on board, groaning. The vessel weaved; Miru's sister could not keep it on bearing.

Despite her weakness the girl was a natural sailor. Many years ago Marama had predicted that Renga Roiti would be known for three qualities—wit, speed and love of seabirds. Ia's daughter revealed all those traits on the canoe. She bantered with Miru, making him laugh, helping him forget the madness of their goal for a while. In spite of Marama's call and his new burden, for Renga Roiti he was still the same freckle-faced brother whose head had been splattered by bird dung.

She moved nimbly on board; soon she could rig sails and climb the mast. She sprawled on the bow in order to sight dolphins, sharks, tuna and spouting whales. She swung on the rigging and swayed by one hand, scanning the skies for sea swallows, albatross and diving gannets. She watched especially for her friends the sacred terns, who went out to sea at dawn and flew homeward at death-light. When she saw them, she cried out with joy. Te Rahai and Miru could hear her high-pitched calls above the hissing of their bow and the sound of wind driving their sail.

In all his years the old seaman had never seen anyone move on a boat like red-haired Renga Roiti, nor had he ever seen a sailor with vision so sharp. Yet the girl did not have the strength to paddle their outrigger through the surf, to hold a course in a current, to set the sail or tighten the ropes in a stiff breeze.

Te Rahai presented his grandchildren to a pair of shipbuilders, two of the last on Vaitéa. They were men who in their youth had seen mighty stands of great-palms, the trees that once provided heartwood for houses and vessels in the fleet. The old sailors showed Miru and Renga Roiti how to build a dugout canoe.

First they felled a sandalwood tree, trimmed and hollowed it. They left the wood to dry for a few days in the sun. Then the builders laid down a keel. Before lashing them together with vines of hibiscus, they carved planks and prowboards. With powder of shell-lime and ochre, mixed with moss and rainwater, they caulked, primed and painted the hull.

The shipbuilders helped the children to set their new craft afloat in the harbor. Together Miru and Renga Roiti sailed along the shore. She relished being alone with him. By now she was beginning to see the changes in her brother, who was not the same boy who had once played with her and Kenetéa.

Knowing that time pressed, Te Rahai let his grandchildren sail his two-hulled canoe on open water. It had once been the most seaworthy longboat on Vaitéa, but the old vessel had not been out for years. Like the early ships in the fleet, its masts, decks, hulls and keels had been hewn from palm wood.

After refitting for short runs Miru, Renga Roiti and their grandfather launched the craft with aid from the two builders. First the three hugged the coast in the big vessel, circling the island in both directions, going with the breeze or tacking against it. Little by little they ventured into the bluewater, where dolphins played along their bows.

Miru still craved to dive and swim with his spirit brothers. But the captain would not allow him; how could Te Rahai manage the twin-hulled boat with only a young girl to assist? The old seaman himself could barely hold a steady rudder. Miru and Renga Roiti wondered who would replace their grandfather as the third member of their crew.

Training those two sailors, Te Rahai's body grew supple, his back straightened, and his eyes turned brighter. He knew the satisfaction of an elder man who has young people in his care, to whom he can offer his experience and knowledge. Aware that he might never sail again, he cherished that time. After all Te Rahai's totem was not a fish, dolphin, whale, seabird, plant, tree or mountain. It was the slippery path of death, altar of the world, the ocean itself.

For Miru and Renga Roiti the days went fast. They watched and listened, learning eagerly, all eyes and ears. They revered and loved their teacher. As the children sailed and spent more time together, they grew fonder of each other too. Renga Roiti had almost forgiven Miru for abandoning her in favor of the dark-haired girl from the other tribe.

The old captain trained brother and sister to sleep in snatches, like babies, in order to stay alert. He instructed them to gauge an island's proximity from subtle land currents or cloud banks that piled up in the afternoons. He showed them other arts that he had learned in his years on the water. Te Rahai even warned them about the music that mariners hear when they are lost at sea and lose their minds.

The ocean taught Miru too. It showed him how to hear winds, waves, seabirds' calls and beating wings, how to listen for silences. It taught him to see, to watch the swells, clouds and sun. Renga Roiti admitted that her brother was finally learning to use his eyes well.

The sea also helped Miru to be more patient, to have a quieter heart. It gave him the peace that he had felt in his grandfather's house. It taught him how little he was on the ocean, wide as the wind. It did not teach him how to forget his father, who had never been at war so long, nor white-armed Kenetéa.

When he was not in a boat, he waited for the girl to return to their meeting place. Tides rose and fell. One day at death-light he spotted her standing by their cove. The air shimmered, and Miru felt a flutter in his chest.

He approached and greeted Kenetéa. The girl appeared taller, more shapely since he had seen her last. Where she had splashed in the foam a light down glistened on her arms. Miru breathed an aroma he had not smelled before—earth and flowers, the wind blowing off the sea and through her dark hair.

As he held her waist with both hands, he rubbed noses with Kenetéa. She looked down: her long, black eyelashes made two small half-moons against the paleness of her cheeks. She glanced up quickly, and the whites flashed in her eyes.

"Téa," he said, using the nickname that no one else knew.

She grinned. "Ru." He loved the sound of his secret name on her lips.

He gazed at her. "I see little seeds at the center of your eyes."

Kenetéa startled. "You're the only one besides my mother who sees them. She calls them drops of the moon." Both stood still, staring into each other's eyes.

A breaking roller woke them from their reverie. "How did you cross the border?" Miru asked.

"I braided my hair like yours and disguised myself." With one hand she skimmed her black tresses, shiny as a tern's wing. Kenetéa wore a tapa cloth, stained yellow with turmeric, the color of Miru's tribe. "Next I waited for a lull in the fighting and sneaked over the line. I wanted to see you." When she had finished speaking, as though she would say more, Kenetéa's lips remained open. The light of the setting sun shone on their moist surface and her small white teeth.

She examined the new marks on Miru's face, shoulders and chest. As she observed him, her eyes seemed to have a brilliance of their own, beyond the sun's light. Yet they were blacker than the knives of obsidian that men used to kill each other.

"I like your tattoos," she told him. With her fingers Kenetéa stroked the images of dolphins on Miru's chest, the blue and red lines on his face. A current like the shock of an eel ran down to his toes.

She sat on the sand with her knees drawn up to her chin, her toes in the lapping water. Miru squatted beside her. Around them shadows deepened.

"Marama told me to forget you," he said.

"Why?"

"Because my tribe's at war with yours. Also because she wants me to make a voyage to another island."

Kenetéa whirled toward Miru, and a wavy lock of her hair brushed his face. "Why?"

Miru studied the tattoos of great-palm and hibiscus on the girl's chest. "To bring back seeds and young trees to save the forests on Vaitéa."

Beyond the surf the ocean heaved. "I would miss you so much, Ru," she said. Kenetéa paused. "But Marama knows. Our land, woods and our seas are sick," she said, touching the images of trees on her chest. She spoke in a tone that Miru had not heard before; she sounded more like a woman than a girl.

He rose on his knees. "Do you mean you want me to go?"

Kenetéa was watching the sky where the evening star had appeared in the west. "Only you could make that trip, Ru—nearly all men are at war or have died in battle. You've been spared because you're too young to be a soldier. Marama's chosen you." As her eyes followed a comet shooting across the sky, she said, "You'll have to wait until you've undergone the last rite of manhood."

Miru lowered his eyes. "I'm going to receive Marama's call, Téa."

"How long will the voyage take?"

"Maybe half a year. If we return."

Kenetéa paused before replying. "You will return, I know. Who else is in the crew?"

"Only Renga Roiti for now. We're still searching for a third sailor."

"I didn't know that girls or women were allowed."

"So far there's nobody else."

She hesitated. "Could you make the journey in the name of both tribal gods, Tangaroa and Makemake? It might help to make peace on our island." Kenetéa stood slowly. "Ru, there's something I want to tell you."

He sprang to his feet. "What?"

When she turned to him, Kenetéa's look was dark, deep as memory. "In three days I must go to the white virgins' cave at Ana o Keke."

Miru remembered sighting that distant site from his canoe— perched on a towering cliff, veiled in fog, waves pounding on the rocks below. "Why?"

"My mother and father have prepared me. They've kept me out of the sun so my skin would stay fair."

"Is that why you always come here at sunset or on cloudy days?"

"Yes." The ocean breathed through Kenetéa's voice.

Miru stepped closer. "Téa, I'll go to see you there before we sail."

She smiled. "Silly Ru, don't you know that boys and men are banned from the virgins' cave? The taboo grove around it is patrolled by lookouts and soldiers." Kenetéa paused again. "I will be sad without you."

As if she had placed her hand inside of Miru's chest, those words gripped the boy's heart. "How long will you be gone, Téa?"

"Three years from my first moon-days."

Miru recalled the last time they had met in the cove, when she had told him about her bleeding. "I can't wait so long," he said.

Kenetéa nudged him. Miru felt a current shoot from his chest to his toes. "Impatient leaping dolphin," she called him. "Your voyage will help to make the time pass."

He ignored those words. "Do you want to go to Ana o Keke?"

"No—I don't want to be so far from you." Kenetéa's high, small breasts rose and fell with her quickened breathing. "But you'll be away for months and I must obey my mother and father."

"What will happen to you in the cave?"

She lowered her eyes. "It's the same for girls in both tribes," she said, "Raas or Tuus. The guardians will keep us out of the sunlight, bathe us, comb our hair, dye our skin with red clay. Other things."

"What things?"

"I cannot tell you. Only women know about them."

Miru blurted, "At least we can spend the next three days together!"

Brave Kenetéa tried to laugh. "Tomorrow the king and his priests will come to bless the new white virgins." She stared at the horizon. "On the second day we'll travel there. On the third we'll enter the cave."

The petals of her lips trembled as she finished speaking. Miru felt an urge to lick the saliva from Kenetéa's mouth. He pressed his face to hers, rubbed noses and kissed her deeply.

The girl was too surprised to react. She caught her breath, her pale skin flushed, and she stepped back from Miru. "Remember the woods, fields and shore when I'm gone," Kenetéa told him. "The places where we've been. Remember, Ru, they're all one."

Gracefully she turned and walked away. In the gathering darkness he watched her fade from his sight. Streams of tears flowed from Miru's eyes.

For three days the sun did not shine. Rain poured and cloaked Vaitéa in a shroud. Drooping trees wept on the forest floor. During those long, dreary days Miru tried to relive the childhood of his joy that he had known with Kenetéa. He wandered on the coast, in fields and woodlands, over hills, seeking the spots where they had gone together. He would have liked to retrieve all the footsteps they had taken and keep them always.

Those places did not console him. They only wound the heartstrings tighter in Miru's chest. On the shore he listened for the sweet music of his childhood; he did not hear the old songs of the wind, trees and waves. Instead he heard the breeze sighing, "Vaitéa . . . Kenetéa . . . Vaitéa." He felt an ocean of sorrow.

The girl's absence made him do things he would regret. Miru squashed bugs, uprooted herbs and flowers, slashed young hibiscus and toromiro trees with his knife of obsidian.

One afternoon he ran up the sides of the volcano of Rano Kau, then down a sheer path to the sea. He kicked pebbles, stones, rocks and sticks ahead of him. They rolled downhill and tumbled into the surf.

On a ledge Miru came upon a large colony of white gannets. He spotted a male who was performing the breeding dance for a pair of hens. The bird lifted each foot in turn, extended both wings and raised its head in rapture, making a long, yearning cry. Miru stalked the gannet from behind, seized it by the neck and plunged his knife into its breast.

As the bird died in his hands, he looked at its eyes. They saw straight into the boy—the black waters, the tangled woods of him. When the light departed from those eyes, Miru withdrew his knife slathered in blood. He hurled the warm heap of feathers into the sea.

The gannet's body rose and fell on the waves that sparkled in the late-afternoon sun. If Kenetéa had not left, he knew, he would not have killed the bird. Miru envied the male gannet because it no longer had to search for love. How peaceful it must be to float on the surface, he thought, to sink and lie on the sea bottom. If only he could be dead until Kenetéa completed her exile in the virgins' cave.

Clouds scudded across the sky. Miru ached for her. After a full morning of training with Renga Roiti one day, he said goodbye and tugged his outrigger canoe across the beach. He paddled the small craft through high surf. In the open water he rigged a sail of tapa cloth.

A breeze grew, waves swelled, currents tossed the little boat. Miru tacked to the north, skirting the headland of Ana o Keke. He surveyed the jagged point where the ocean seethed and breakers crashed, spewing foam into the air. If he tried to swim to land, he would be dashed on the rocks, and even if he survived, he could not have climbed the precipice that soared straight up from the coast. Miru called out the girl's name: "Ke-ne-té-a!" The cliff face echoed: ". . . é-a . . . é-a . . . ," scarcely audible above the screaming wind and rollers booming on the crags. High above on the crest, where fog swirled, he glimpsed a girl whose long, black hair was blowing in the gale.

Chapter 4

Crossings

One morning when the seas were too high to sail, Miru slipped away from the great-house. At a crossroads two dwarves burst into his life.

"I'm Kuihi!" piped one.

The boy assumed a defensive crouch.

"I'm Kuaha!" chimed the other.

They had sprung out of nowhere. Miru glanced around him: there was not a bush, tree or rock where the dwarves could have taken cover in the dawn light. He felt abashed for being caught unawares, forgetting the warrior's vigilance his father had taught him.

The first called, "Son of Ia!"

"Son of Koro!" cried the other.

The boy relaxed: what harm could come from these two dwarves who were familiar with his family, who hardly reached his waist? Miru saw that the two creatures were twins. He contemplated Kuihi—red hair and goatee—and Kuaha—black hair and beard. One side of their heads was braided in the Tuu style, while the other had straight locks like the Raas. Tufts of hair sprouted from their pointed ears; the lobes were pierced with wooden lizards. Tattoos of the same animal covered their limbs and torso.

"Are you Raas or Tuus?" he asked them.

They smirked, reminding Miru of lizards sunning themselves on a rock. Then they turned toward each other.

"Are we Tuus?" the first queried.

The other inquired, "Are we Raas?"

The dwarves spun on their heels, skipped a few steps, did three handsprings, landed on their feet and whirled around.

Kuaha cried, "Follow me, Miru of the dolphins!"

Kuihi called, "Miru of the freckles, come with me!"

The brothers cavorted down the road. Both halted, looked back, winked at Miru, cartwheeled in the dust. They led him to a sparse wood where they stopped to unbraid his dark-brown hair and dress him in new clothes, dyed red in the Raas' tribal color. The dwarves did not bother to disguise themselves. Miru wondered how they guessed that he planned to cross into the hostile land.

As stealthy as wild animals they guided him to the border. The three skirted enemy scouts, crawled and reached a low, rounded hill above the valley where Kenetéa's family lived. While Kuihi and Kuaha stood watch, the boy knelt, concealed by the bushes, looking down at the great-house she had shown him one day when the tribes were still at peace. As quickly as they had appeared, the twins vanished.

Miru smiled to himself as he waited, recalling the dwarves, happy to be within sight of Kenetéa's home. Soon he saw a woman pass over the threshold on her way to a well, where she began to wash clothes on the stone lip. Dogs played in the grass around her feet, and pigs scavenged in the dust.

Miru walked down the gentle hill to the house. As the woman scrubbed, her black hair swirled around her head. For an instant he imagined she was Kenetéa.

When he drew closer, the dogs barked. The lady turned slowly.

"I know your daughter," Miru announced.

"Then you must know she's gone."

"Yes. I love Kenetéa and miss her deeply."

"Many love her," she said calmly. "Who are you?"

"Miru, Koro's son."

The woman gasped when she recognized the enemy warrior's name. "I shouldn't be talking to the son of a Tuu soldier. If my husband or the Raa troops found you here, they'd kill you."

"I'd rather die than live without her."

The woman studied Miru's haggard countenance. "You already look half-dead, young man." Bees and flies buzzed around them.

"Nobody loves Kenetéa more than I do."

"I can see that in your eyes. They'd be a lovely green if they weren't so bloodshot."

"I know her better than anyone else."

The lady smiled. "More than her own mother?"

"You and I are the only ones who've seen the moon-drops in her eyes." The woman gave a start when she heard Miru's words. He did not alter the grave expression on his face. "Kenetéa told me that she must stay in the virgins' cave for three years. I cannot wait so long."

She stared at him. "If more Tuu boys loved our daughters like you," she said, "maybe their fathers wouldn't try to kill us." Glancing toward the hill, the woman added, "I also miss Kenetéa. And my husband—he's away at war again." Tears welled in her dark eyes. "I'm going to fix something to heal our sadness. My name is Neira."

She spread the moist clothes on the stone well's lip and walked over the threshold of her great-house. In the sunlight Miru waited. Butterflies floated in the air.

A child skipped from the door. His hair was shiny and black like Kenetéa's; his ears bulged from his head. He gaped at Miru.

"I know the constellations by heart," the boy said in a voice like a song. "But I've never seen as many stars as the freckles on your face." Miru laughed for the first time since Kenetéa had gone. The child squinted in the sunlight. "What's your name?" he asked the visitor.

"Miru." The boy arched his eyebrows; he had never heard such a name. "And you're Mohani, right?"

"How did you know?"

"Your sister told me."

"I miss Kenetéa." Yes, Miru thought. "My spirit brothers are mulberry and coconut trees," the child said, pointing to the woods beyond the house. "Who are yours?"

"Leaping dolphins."

Mohani looked askance at the outsider. "Only Tuus have totems from the sea." He paused, intrigued. He had never spoken to anyone from the other tribe. The boy had a vague feeling that he was doing something wrong. "How old are you?" he asked Miru.

"Fifteen summers. To judge by your great knowledge, you must be at least that age."

Kenetéa's brother did not smile. "I'm ten—almost." Renga Roiti's age, Miru told himself, thinking how much older his sister seemed.

Mohani observed the visitor's tattoos. "Have you passed the final test of manhood?"

Neira's return saved Miru from answering the child. In her hands she carried two cups carved of toromiro wood. She offered one to the newcomer and kept the other for herself: "Drink the cup of first meeting," she told him.

"We don't have this custom," Miru responded. "I like it." He drank. The potion tasted of roots and earth, bitter as his memory of Marama's cave.

The libation did not heal his pain. After leaving the enemies' land, Miru pined for Kenetéa as much as ever. Between sailings with Renga Roiti he hazarded more excursions to see Neira and her son. Each time the two dwarves appeared exactly when he needed their assistance to range the no-man's land between the tribes.

Miru took pleasure in being with the woman and Mohani, whose black hair, gestures and movements reminded him of Kenetéa. Before descending into the valley he and the dwarves always perused the zone in case the woman's husband had returned. "Raunui is a true warrior," the twins warned in a tone that Miru had never heard in their voices. "When he steps on the battlefield, his enemies feel a blast of wind."

One day Miru asked Neira about the dwarves. She smiled. "The truth is that nobody's sure where they were born," she explained, "where they live, who they are. Some people think they're *aku-aku*, spirits of our island who've always been here. Still others say the twins sprang from the mire where lizards breed." Neira paused. "A few believe they're messengers of a certain Tuu priestess." The woman saw the question on her visitor's face. He did not ask if the dwarves were envoys of Marama.

Miru helped the woman fill the empty places in her heart, the monotony of days without her husband and daughter. At first he was jealous of Mohani, who had lived under the same roof as Kenetéa. But when he looked into the boy's eyes, he saw hers there too—black, shinier than obsidian. Miru relented. He rubbed noses with Mohani and played with him as he used to play with Renga Roiti and Kenetéa, before he left his sister and their friends for the dark-haired girl. Still the child was wary of the outsider with the odd name and a totem spirit from the sea.

Neira was daughter to a rongorongo master, a singer of tales who had been deeply schooled in the wisdom of the past. Sometimes she sang or told stories to Miru and her son. Mohani learned them by heart. The boy also knew starsongs, ancestor-lines, poems and legends taught him by his grandfather. Ia's son had not met anyone with a memory like Mohani's.

Miru decided it was time to tell Neira about the voyage. He expected her to react with disbelief, like everyone else on the island. But she merely said, "I know, son."

"How?"

"Our men are at war but a few women from the tribes stay in touch with each other. We're aware that our forests and our seas are sick." Miru recalled Kenetéa's words. "We must heal them in order to survive," Neira said. "Your quest for seeds and shoots of new trees may help us. Why else would I allow you to visit our great-house?"

"I'll miss Kenetéa terribly."

"You miss her already, before you've even set sail. You must forget her." Miru lowered his head, and his green eyes moistened. Neira stroked his hair with long, white fingers that resembled her daughter's. "Hatred between the tribes is growing fiercer," she said. The woman paused. "Some of our soldiers have been forced to sacrifice their own children for mingling with the enemy. If my husband learned that Kenetéa had been with you, he might be shamed into killing her."

"No!" he cried. Neira's utterance was like a lance in Miru's breast. He turned away to hide the tears brimming from his eyes.

"Raunui's a tender husband and father," she said. "How he loves his children! But he's a warlord of our tribe whose life is not his own." Kenetéa's mother placed her hands on Miru's shoulders, which were shaking as he wept. "I have some better news for you."

She waited for Miru to compose himself. With tears still streaming down his cheeks, wiping them with both hands, he looked hopefully at Neira. "I've received a message from the priestess at Kote Pora," she told him.

"You know Marama?"

"I met her when the tribes were living in peace. She's sent me a message by runner. Listen, Miru. The sorceress wants me to teach you how to harvest, sow and plant seeds, shoots and saplings so you'll be prepared for your mission and your return."

"I haven't even accepted her call."

"Often she knows things before they've happened." Neira looked at the ground. "Miru, how do you expect to complete a voyage that nobody's made before?"

"I like the impossible."

"I knew that."

"Will you show me how to plant and harvest?"

Neira paused while Miru searched her face. The woman's skin was the color of moonlight, like Kenetéa's but a little duller, lined with a few wrinkles. She smiled. "There are no young trees to harvest here, but if you're crazy enough to go on such an expedition, I'll teach you the rest."

"Will you also show my sister? She'll be in my crew."

"I thought it was forbidden for a girl to sail on a longboat." Miru did not reply. "How old is she?"

"Ten summers."

Neira's eyes opened wide: "You're going to travel across the seas with a girl my son's age?" Miru remained silent, and wind gusted around them. "Who else will sail with you?"

"We haven't found a third crewman."

Neira sighed. "If you're fated to die, how can I stop it? So I'll teach you and your sister what I know. But be careful, son! If my husband finds out, we'll all be in danger."

The next day he guided Renga Roiti to the border. As they approached the line, he informed her about Kuihi and Kuaha, who appeared as opportunely as ever. While the twins dressed and disguised both sister and brother, they charmed the girl, joking with her, making her laugh so hard that she forgot her apprehension of entering Raa lands. Once their charges had reached the hill above the valley, Kuihi and Kuaha disappeared.

Miru presented his sister to Neira, who treated her like the daughter she missed sorely. The woman escorted Ia's children to the only stand of trees that still grew in the valley. Mohani brought up the rear.

Kenetéa's mother pointed to the spindly trees that somehow had escaped being felled for firewood or weapons. On that day and others, when the seas were too rough for Miru and Renghi to launch the twin-hulled canoe, Neira taught them to pick or collect seeds, to separate young sprigs from their trunks, to moisten and pull saplings gently from the earth. She showed brother and sister how to prepare a bed by clearing, turning, leveling the soil and digging rows. She taught them to soften seeds by soaking them in a calabash filled with rainwater, to plant them by mounding and covering them with dried grass, to shield them from the wind by circling them with rocks, to weed and water, to set and space the shoots and seedlings, to thin and prune.

Mohani always tagged along. Since Miru also had a father at war, he understood the child. For his part Mohani was becoming less suspicious of the stranger.

Neira's son took to Renga Roiti, who delighted in playing with a boy her age. She forgave him for being Kenetéa's brother. She told him stories about birds of the land, sea and air, entrancing him with their calls: "Eee! Pi-ru-ru! Ka-ara-ara! Te vero-vero! Kava-eo-eo!" In turn Mohani sang her the ancestor-lines and starsongs he had learned from his grandfather. The two children became fast friends. For Renga Roiti he was her "little brother" and her "sea swallow." He called her "Renghi," the nickname that only Miru had used before.

One night Ia's children sat on the beach, watching the wake of a quarter moon glittering on the sea. Their bellies rumbled.

"We must depart soon," Miru said.

"Before we die of hunger."

"And before the season changes." He gnawed his lips. "We still need a third crewman."

"Don't worry, Ru."

His nostrils flared, and he turned on Renga Roiti: "Where did you learn that name?"

The girl startled. Looking away and blushing, she said, "I overheard Kenetéa use it a long time ago."

"Don't call me that again." Waves lapped the shore.

"Anyway I've found him," Renga Roiti said.

"Who?"

The girl wavered before speaking. "The third member of our crew."

"Who is he?"

"Mohani."

Miru's laugh almost reached the moon. "He's a Raa and he's never seen the ocean! Anyway he's not strong enough to sail a ship."

"He'll grow stronger with time."

"What time? We have to leave before the next moon's full."

"You and Te Rahai can train him."

"That would delay our voyage until the season of bad weather. Storms would sink our boat."

"Mohani's grandfather taught him starsongs that could help us navigate at night. He forgets nothing," Renga Roiti said. "His memory's like a clam."

"I know. But Neira would never allow him to go. She already has a daughter and a husband away from home."

"I'll try to persuade her."

Miru considered. "And if Mohani's father learned we were taking his son, the man would try to kill us."

"Raunui would do that anyhow—because you've talked to Kenetéa." In Renga Roiti's voice he heard the old resentment, her jealousy of the Raa girl. "You've broken all the taboos," she told him. "You've been with her, you've met Raunui's wife and played with his son, trespassing on his home and his land."

"Suppose he doesn't manage to kill us first," Miru said, "and Neira gives us her permission. What makes you think Mohani would sail with us?"

"He likes me. Didn't I tell you not to worry?"

Miru watched the thin moon's reflection on the night-sea. He imagined himself wandering over endless oceans with a pair of children for a crew, farther and farther from thin-ankled Kenetéa.

One afternoon they found Neira squatting on the ground at the threshold of her house, where she was skinning a yam. Renga Roiti looked knowingly at her brother before going inside to play with Mohani.

"All my loves have been taken away," Neira confided in Miru. "My daughter's in the white virgins' cave, my husband's at war. Now my son will sail on a journey to nowhere. I'll be alone." Renghi's already convinced her, Miru said to himself.

Neira wept. One of her tears dripped onto the obsidian blade of her knife, where it shone like a dark pearl.

He stepped closer and placed his hands on the woman's black tresses. Miru recalled Kenetéa's hair. "Why are you letting Mohani go?"

Neira dropped her knife to the ground, keeping the yam in her palm. "Because this root is all we have left to eat. Yam yesterday, yam today," she moaned, "tomorrow nothing."

"Yams are so scarce in our territory that only warriors are allowed to eat them."

"It may become the same in our lands. It's not the food alone, Miru. Our great-house is cold. I'd have to chop our last trees to cook, to heat the rooms—and you know I would never do that. I can't feed my own son or keep him warm. Can you imagine how that makes a mother feel?" Miru nodded, thinking of Ia. "I'm also letting Mohani go because new trees might heal our island," Neira resumed, "even help to stop the wars between our tribes. He knows starsongs better than anyone since my father died. His spirit brothers are coconut and mulberry, two of the trees that have almost died out on Vaitéa."

She paused. "And I'm allowing my son to go because *she* chose the great-palm and hibiscus as her totems—two more trees you're supposed to find on your quest." When he heard the names of Kenetéa's spirits, Miru felt a pull on his heart, aware that the woman was speaking of her daughter. Neira glanced away. "It's what she would wish," the mother said, wiping her eyes on one arm. "And Mohani himself has agreed to join the voyage—for his sister and for me. He understands." She looked up at Miru. "Marama has sent me another message."

"What?"

"Be careful!" she cried, gaping at him with her dark eyes. "Raunui knows you've been here."

Miru shuddered when he heard the name of Kenetéa's father. "How did he learn?"

"Mohani let it slip out the last time my husband returned from the wars—the child's too innocent to know the danger." She paused. "Raunui also knows our daughter has crossed the border to visit you."

Miru looked astounded. "Who told him?"

"I can't reveal that, son."

"You said some warriors sacrificed their children who consorted with the enemy. Neira, would your husband ever kill Kenetéa?"

The woman burst into tears. "Not if you leave the island now, Miru!" She spread her arms. "Please go and promise to bring my son back."

"I will, Neira."

If tall Ihu had been there, with his nose like a bowsprit, he would been amused by the confidence of a young man who had never captained a longboat. But Miru had more doubts than ever. For the second time he felt the burden of his call, like the weight of a forest on his shoulders. Many lives depended on him. His childhood and his love seemed to have disappeared.

Mohani whimpered as he said farewell to his mother. Miru and Renga Roiti led the boy to the border, where she braided his hair in Tuu style, and the three changed into clothes dyed yellow with turmeric. Like any other child he enjoyed a disguise. They ran over fields and woods to reach Koro's great-house.

The next morning Miru found his sister and the boy seated by the well.

"We've just visited Te Rahai," she said. "Maybe you should talk to him also."

He walked across the dusty square to the old captain's house. Seated alone, his grandfather was staring at the hearth in the longroom.

Te Rahai looked up. "Mohani's a weakling, Miru. He's never seen the ocean, much less sailed on it. But he chanted the starsongs for me. His memory's as good as his grandfather's, who was one of the last singers trained in the rope of knowledge. He can recite those songs backward and forward—I've never heard anyone like him. They could help you steer at night on the outward voyage." Te Rahai paused. "And if you found another island, the starsongs would make it easier to follow a reverse course to Vaitéa. Besides there's nobody else but Mohani. And the boy desires to travel. You'll have to teach him as I've taught you and your sister. I'm too frail."

Miru heard pain in Te Rahai's words, saw it in his mouth and eyes. "Grandfather," he said, "we don't have time to train Mohani. You know we must set out shortly. If we wait we'll grow weaker from hunger and

Mohani's father will track him and kill us. Even if we survived to make the journey, the summer storms would smash our canoe to pieces."

Gazing at the cold ashes in the hearth, the old man did not reply. Miru caressed his shoulder and left him alone there.

Brother and sister took Mohani to the shore. They taught him water games learned by all Tuu children. The winter sea was cold, and Kenetéa's brother panicked in the surf.

"Why do I have to swim?" he cried, sputtering water. "My totems are trees—not a fish or seabird. I only want to recite the starpaths and be a rongorongo master."

Miru looked into those black pupils, seeing Kenetéa's there. He felt pity for the boy and strove to be patient. Cuffing Mohani on the head, he told him, "Your ears are so big that you could float on them."

"And your face looks like a hill of ants," the child retorted.

Renga Roiti smiled. If another boy had said those words to her brother, he would have paid for it.

Within a few days Mohani began to lose his fear of wading near the shore. Miru and Renga Roiti took him to sea in the outrigger canoe. As soon as they pitched through the first swells, Mohani turned sick and vomited over the side. But he learned easily the names of currents and winds, stars and constellations, many of them familiar from his grandfather's stories. The boy had almost found his sea legs.

Te Rahai aided the three children in launching the twin-hulled vessel. He did not board himself, knowing the young people would have to learn to sail the large ship by themselves. It would be the last step in the crew's preparation for their journey.

On the first sorties Miru held the steering paddle while his sister and Mohani tried to work the sheets. The boy's hands were too small to grasp the thick cordage. Then the two children took turns at the helm. Renga Roiti managed to steer in smooth waters, but she was not strong enough to hold a course in choppy seas; Mohani's fingers failed to reach around the rudder's handle. Miru had to stay at the tiller while the girl and boy wrestled with the ropes.

Following starpaths, they ran on a flat ocean for days and nights. Miru led them as far as Motiro, the sole scrap of land between Vaitéa and the sea-waste, a barren rock that was the wind's home. Renga Roiti and Mohani proved they could sail on open waters in calm weather.

Winter had drawn to an end, and spring arrived on Vaitéa. Ihu, priest of the tribe, convened the family in the longroom. All came except Koro, who still had not returned.

"Many changes will come to pass during the long expedition," graceful Ia told them. "Renga Roiti may have her first moon-blood. Although the time for my daughter's seclusion hasn't arrived, we should make an exception for her. It's what Koro would have wished. She must be confined for tattooing." Renghi's smile beamed from one ear to the other.

During the next few days a *maori* or artist traced tattoos on her limbs and torso. In addition to Renga Roiti's winged sister—the sooty tern drawn across her chest and shoulders—he adorned her with leaves and branches of sacred sandalwood, one of the trees that were vanishing on Vaitéa. She was the first girl or boy of her tribe to have them incised on her body. Renghi bore the pain of the needles as bravely as any young man.

Ia's daughter was released from seclusion. Renga Roiti felt so proud of her tattoos! She looked a bit older, more aware: what her wise mother had wanted.

Renghi was restless to depart. She could not imagine failure. "My big brother Miru knows the sea," she told everyone, "and my little brother Mohani knows the starpaths. Together they'll lead us to a new island. They and my birds, of course," she added proudly. Miru's heart tensed: his sister reminded him of a flying fish who rises in the air to escape a shark without knowing if others lurk where it slips back into the water.

Mohani lacked Renghi's faith in herself and their captain. Although he enjoyed the care and attention of Miru's family, the boy missed his parents. He did not feel fully at home among a strange tribe. Staring at the ceiling of reeds and stalks of sugarcane in the great-house, turning fitfully, Mohani could not sleep through the nights.

The two old mariners helped them construct a windward shelter on the ship's deck. There one of the young people could rest or eat while the other two sailed the boat. The men also aided brother, sister and Mohani in securing a sandbox forward on the opposite deck, where a fire could burn in dry weather, keep the crew warm and cook their food.

The shipbuilders cut prowboards and sternposts from a beached canoe. They carved them in the form of a giant bird's double head and tail, then fastened them to the twin-hulled craft. They inspected, repaired and cleaned paddles, bailers, the two masts, the sails of tapa and rigging of rope and vines. They re-caulked the vessel's seasoned heartwood with sap and pitch, painted it with new pigments of shell-lime and ochre. The ship was ready.

Chapter 5

Marama

Early in the morning he left for Kote Pora. He heard sounds of battle on the way—shrieks, howls, clashing of armor and weapons. When Miru reached the forbidden grove, once the densest woods on Vaitéa, he saw just a few scraggly trees.

Identifying Koro's son, the guard allowed him to pass. Miru turned to take a last look at the sky and clouds. His mouth felt dry, and he knew the dread of all boys who arrived for the ceremony. If I don't pass the rite, he worried, how will I tell my family and my tribesmen, how will I face Kenetéa—if I ever see her again?

When Miru crawled into the cave, three young women received him. Each carried a torch of dried bark soaked in fish fat. The attendants smiled at him: he recognized the faces of girls with whom he had played as a child, transformed by time and knowledge. One's hair was black like obsidian, another's red, the third's brown like his own. Around their narrow waists they wore only a belt of tapa cloth. Smeared with coconut oil, their bodies shimmered in the torchlight. How could Miru fail to recall Kenetéa? The three women exuded a fragrance of turmeric that lingered in the boy's nostrils.

They conducted him through twisting passages. To avoid bumping the stone ceiling Miru lowered his head. They reached a lofty chamber, where he saw pieces of sky framed by small round holes in the cavern's ceiling.

53

Two of the women quenched their torches while the third hung hers on the cave wall. As they left the chamber, the three oiled bodies seemed to swim away like fish in a shoal. Waves beat the crags below.

"Welcome, son of Ia and Koro," a voice declared behind him as the torch died. Knowing Marama's winged words, he swung to face her. "I was sure you would return," she said, laughing. With her sharp fingernails she scraped Miru's cheeks. "You still have a boy's freckles." By now he was used to the witch's power of seeing clearly without light.

Marama slid her fingers down his neck, one shoulder and arm, his waist. With a cold, wet hand she grabbed Miru's wrist. He felt the same repugnance as the first time in the cave.

Hobbling, Marama led him down a corridor. They crossed a portal into a higher room lit by a torch. Beneath the light a stone altar smoked with herbs, two conch shells on its surface.

The priestess invited Miru to sit on a reed mat. He squatted there. Marama limped to her chair, hewn from wood of the toromiro tree, whose arms and legs were fashioned with creatures from land, sea and air—snakes, turtles, seals, fish, lobsters, birds. Miru peered at the woman's face, round like the moon. On her head she wore her tall cone of feathers.

"I want to be a man now," he told Marama.

"You'll be a man when you give up your love for Kenetéa, when you pass the final test and follow my mission." Miru pictured the young girl in his mind. As though she could see his thoughts, Marama said, "Your love for Kenetéa is marked by death—our people are at war."

Miru tried to hold back the tears welling in his eyes. "You're an old woman," he said. "How can you understand my love for her?"

Marama's lips bent upward in a smile. "Don't talk to me about love!" she cried, gripping Miru's arm. With her free hand she struck her breastbone. "You're too young to know what this heart has felt."

"But you're not me, old one. How can you know what I feel?"

"Nor are you me, boy-child. So how can you be sure I don't know what you feel?"

Miru smiled to himself. It was useless to have words with Marama.

"Hear me!" the seer commanded. "If Kenetéa's father knew that you've touched her body, that you've trespassed on his tribal lands, crossed the threshold of his great-house and spoken to his wife and son, he'd stalk and kill you. And do you know what Raunui would do with your corpse?" Marama did not wait for a reply. "First he'd hang it from a tree for birds to pick your flesh. Then he'd cut off your head, slice it open like a coconut, suck out the brains, etch his clan-signs on your skull and present it to your father." The boy shivered while Marama caught her breath. "Next Raunui and his soldiers would slay Koro and do the same to his body and head. Finally they'd deliver their double prize to your mother and sister before raping, slaughtering and stringing them on trees too."

Miru's heart raced and his temples pounded. He burned with all the rage of his fifteen years—against the sorceress, Raas, the war, Kenetéa's exile.

"One more thing," Marama said.

I don't know if I can hear more, Miru thought, pulling his arm from the witch's grasp. He wondered if the priestess knew what Neira had told him, that Kenetéa's father might be forced to sacrifice his daughter for mingling with a Tuu.

Marama sighed. "Somebody else has spilled it to you, I see." The corners of her mouth rose in the dawn of a smile.

Miru resigned himself: she could penetrate his mind. He thought of Kenetéa and her mother.

Once more the sorceress seized Miru's arm. "The voyage will help you forget the girl and you'll be a hero for our people."

He laughed to himself: the old witch makes it sound so easy! That quest was even more impossible than his love for bright-eyed Kenetéa. In this I know more than Marama, he thought. Now I'm the adult and she's the child.

"But I'm the one who makes men out of boys," the seer said.

"And I'm the one who has to lead a journey for men."

Yes, thought the priestess, satisfied that Miru expected to embrace her call. "The time has come," she said with a smile.

Marama made a clicking noise with her mouth. One attendant stepped to the stone altar, where she took a conch shell in each hand. Holding them like offerings, she walked toward Miru, placed them in the boy's upturned palms and retreated into the shadows.

"Drink!" Marama ordered. "You have fifteen summers and you're almost a man."

Inhaling the bitter odor of kava root, Miru raised one of the conchs to his mouth, then the other, drinking deeply from both. Again and again, grinning at Marama between gulps, he lifted and lowered the two vessels.

She saw the same foolish face on every young man who tasted kava at Kote Pora. "Go on drinking from the conchs!" the old woman screamed. "Forget about Vaitéa's troubles while you drown them in kava!"

"You offered it to me."

"Yes, so that you would taste it like a man who has an island's fate in his hands—not a boy with a face like chicken-dung!" Her voice resounded against the cavern walls, so clamorous that it muffled the surf's roar, stunning Miru. He dropped the shells. He felt a lightness he had never known, as if the kava was bubbling in his head.

Suddenly Marama released a laugh. He startled, and the sound rumbled, echoing through the cave, merging with the pounding of breakers on the rocks. "Rise, Miru!" she commanded.

At once the servants appeared on the threshold. Marama directed them to serve another conch shell from the altar. "It contains a secret beverage," she told Miru, "laced with herbs, to prepare the initiate." He drank. The potion spread its flowers through his mind.

Marama instructed the servants to undress him. They removed his cape and belt of tapa cloth. The young women anointed Miru with a balm of pressed coconut meat, combined with fluids from plants, flowers and creatures of the earth, air and ocean. In the torchlight his body glistened. The seer and her helpers guided him to the inmost chamber.

It was a room entered at least once by every male on Vaitéa. Miru felt the fear that all boys knew on the night of a ritual concealed from everyone but Marama, her attendants and the men who had gone before.

That night he had dreams that were sweeter than life, memories sweeter than dreams too. He dreamed or recollected Marama's deep-voiced chants and prayers. Miru recalled or dreamed that he was rolling on the cave floor and floating through winding tunnels, his body warmed by women's caresses. He dreamed or remembered grazing of fingers, entwining of oiled arms and legs until he soared and fell asleep, empty, exhausted.

He woke from a slumber so profound that he thought he was rising from the sea floor. Miru had been transported to the middle chamber, where the altar smoldered. He lay sprawled on his back by Marama's chair. In his mouth he had a taste of earth, sea and salt air. Days seemed to have passed since he arrived in Marama's sanctuary.

The priestess looked down at Miru, swaying her head, rocking her cone of feathers. The large shells tingled on her earlobes. With their eyes lowered, bearing trays of shellfish and conchs filled with kava, the three attendants came. In the torchlight Miru tried to catch the young women's glances. Without looking at him they knelt to serve the foods and drink, stood, paused and withdrew as if they had not shared the ritual in the dark.

"Forget them and eat," Marama said. "They're merely instruments of the passage."

Miru stood, stepped forward and crouched by the trays of food. His body was tired. But he felt a new force in his limbs. He also felt hunger; the night had drained and purged him. Or was it the day?

He devoured raw clams, sea urchins and mussels, still cold and dripping strands of kelp. It was as though he were swallowing the sea and its power. With the food he sipped conchfuls of kava, more wisely now. He smiled and wiggled his toes on the cavern floor.

"Stand, Miru!" The ocean breathed through Marama's words. "You've almost completed the last rite. But for you becoming a man must be more than a ritual in my cave."

"What do you mean, Marama?"

He stood while the seer lifted herself with effort from her chair. "Son of Ia and Koro, listen. Have you watched trees swaying in the wind?"

"Yes."

"Have you seen terns gliding on the breeze?"

"Yes."

"Have you watched dolphins leaping in the ocean?"

Miru smiled. "Of course."

"Do you know that your daughters and sons may not see them?"

"No. I mean yes—I think."

"Sit here," the priestess said, pronouncing each word carefully. Miru squatted on the reed mat in front of her chair again. Marama sat too, took his left hand in hers and stroked it. "Now hear, my son."

The sorceress breathed in, exhaled and spoke her music of words: "The earth and sea and sky were once sacred to our people, Miru. We loved each grain of sand on the beaches, every shining leaf in the woods, every bird on the land or shore, each fish in the ocean, each white thread of mist around our volcanoes and mountains." Marama inhaled a deep breath. "We knew the sap that courses through trees as we knew the blood in our veins. The water in our seas and rivers was like our mothers' milk. Our fathers' breath was the wind. We were part of the land, the air and sea and they were part of us. Do you see?" she inquired, rubbing the initiate's hand.

Those words rang in Miru's head. "Yes," he answered.

"Then the changes began. It was so long ago that nobody can remember how it started—not even the priests or the rongorongo masters, schooled in the stories of our people. The two tribes drew apart. Soon they were fighting each other. The wars destroyed most Tuu lands on the coast and Raa territory in the heartland." A gust of wind from offshore whistled through the grotto. "Our sea-battered island has grown old," Marama said in a weary voice. "We've drawn away from the earth and ocean—we're no longer friends to the world. We've lost our mana, the power that binds us to the soil, sky and sea. Do you understand?"

"Yes."

The seer pressed hard on Miru's hand. "Then why did you squash bugs, uproot herbs and flowers, cut down young trees and kill the gannet with your knife?"

How can she know everything, Miru pondered as his face turned red. "I was angry because Kenetéa was leaving for Ana o Keke."

"Will you harm our plants and creatures again?"

"No."

"You, more than anyone," she warned, "—you must cherish all living things on our island and in our seas."

The torch fluttered. Marama still held Miru's hand. As he listened to her thick breathing above the sea's roar, he felt the woman's moist palm and her jagged claws.

"Miru," she said from her chair, "the truth is so simple that our people are blind to it. Open your eyes to see."

"They're open, Marama."

As though she were speaking to herself, dreamily, the woman said, "Sometimes we have to shut our eyes to see." Marama's voice was tender now: "Our greatest suffering is not from killing each other. It's from killing the ocean and the land. We've razed our forests, slashing them for arms and firewood." Marama sighed. "Birds of the air have lost their nests—our parrots, owls and herons have disappeared. They no longer spread the trees' fruits and seeds across Vaitéa. Without plants and roots to hold our soil, the rains wash it away, leeching its strength." The seer sobbed. "Then the winds blow it to the air. Meanwhile our springs and streams are turning dry," Marama said through tears. "And we've fished out the seas around our shores. That's why you see fewer dolphins—they have to swim farther out to seek schools of fish to feed on."

The old witch knows, Miru marveled. How could she have learned about my spirit brothers, he asked himself, confined in her cave? The torch on the wall sputtered, smoked and died.

Marama released his hand. "Listen closely," the woman said, "to the names of six trees—toromiro, coconut, sandalwood, great-palm, hibiscus and mulberry." She stopped so that those names would lodge in Miru's mind.

Marama's chair squeaked as she rose from it. Her breathing grew heavier. Slowly the sorceress kneeled on the mat in front of Miru, so near that he smelled the kava root on her breath, her odor of ashes and smoke. When she placed her all-seeing fingers on his shoulder, they were clammy like the cave's walls.

Moon-faced Marama kneaded Miru's arm. Next she dropped her hands to his thighs, murmuring spells as if she were conjuring a demon in his bones. "Sweet dolphin," she sang, "without new trees from another island, how will our forests grow?" She moaned. "Where would our birds nest without trees? How would we build canoes, how would we equip them? How would we stay warm in the winter? Without the six trees our island will go to waste, our people will die, the sun and moon will wander in the valleys of the night."

Miru saw himself sailing over empty ocean, traveling farther and farther from Vaitéa, his family and the dark-haired girl.

Marama laughed. "She's in your thoughts still. You can think of Kenetéa, son, but you cannot be with her."

She placed the cold palm of her hand on his forehead. "You've welcomed my call and completed the ritual. I bless you. At last you're a man, Miru." He was staggered to hear those words on Marama's lips. "But many boys grow to be men on our island," she added. "You must be more than the others. You must learn to see the truth."

"How?"

"It's like the spirits who once dwelled in our woods and on our shores." Miru wondered if those beings made the music, the songs of wind, waves and trees he used to hear as a child. "You had to glimpse them by looking sideways," all-knowing Marama said. "One should not not look directly at the sun."

"You always speak in riddles. Where are those spirits now?"

Marama grinned like a naughty girl. "I was just going to tell you when you accused me of speaking in riddles. Those spirits are gone."

"Where?"

"Far away."

"Will they return?"

"Perhaps."

"When?"

Taking one of his hands in hers again, Marama said, "Son of Koro, come with me." That name reminded Miru of how much he missed his father.

The seer led him to a small chamber where a single torch burned. She handed him stone tools for digging, planting and hoeing. She also proffered three precious baskets, woven from the finest rushes in the lake at Rano Kau, split, dried and plaited, then waterproofed with strips of banana bark culled from her secluded grove.

"These are the baskets of my teaching, the rope of wisdom," Marama said. "One for the sea, one for the earth and one for the sky. In them you must store the life-giving shoots and seeds—of toromiro, sacred sandalwood, coconut, great-palm, hibiscus and mulberry."

"Tell me about those trees."

Marama inhaled deeply. "Toromiro burns in earth-ovens to cook our food and warm our hearths. Sweet-smelling sandalwood serves for rituals, for our priests' tablets and rongorongos—without them we could not preserve our knowledge of the past. Coconut trees bear fruit for meat, milk and oil." Marama paused to catch her breath. "Great-palms supply timber for houses and canoes. Hibiscus trees give us vines to rig our boats. And mulberries provide bark-cloth for our ships' sails, for handlines, fishing nets and garments to cover our bodies. Those are the six trees you must bring back to Vaitéa."

"Is that all?"

Marama guffawed. "That is enough, Miru."

"How do you know I'll find all those trees on another island?"

"Because you have to. If you fail, we're lost." The surf hissed outside. "You must find the trees, snip their shoots, pull their saplings and place them with their seeds in the vessel's hold. When you return home, you must plant them in our soil." Marama's voice grew louder. "They will grow and someday new forests will cover Vaitéa. The birds of the air will return, spread the seeds and pollinate our trees and flowers. Streams will run in their beds. Sweet dew will fall from the sky. The land will heal and our people will thrive again!"

"What about the spirits?"

"Did you think I'd forgotten? When you accomplish your task, they'll return to our woods and shores."

As if to uphold their new charge, Miru's shoulders straightened: he felt the weight, the urgency of his quest. "Goodbye, Marama," he said. He turned to leave the cave.

The old priestess could not resist the temptation of pronouncing the last words. "May the gods and goddesses watch over you, Miru."

Chapter 6

Quest

The loading of the boat took a full day and night. Miru, Renga Roiti and Mohani tied wooden bowls to the decks for catching rain. Next to them they set reed cages for the last fowl from the people's henhouses. In the windward shelter the crew placed shoots of wild herbs and cuts of sugarcane for their early meals, packed lovingly in strips of bark by Ia. Below decks they stored giant calabashes of fresh water and their staples: sliced banana pulp cured in the sun, wrapped in leaves and bound in fibers, and smoked great-shark prepared by Te Rahai in a way that only he and the shipbuilders knew. During the first days of the passage the voyagers would eat better than the people on Vaitéa, who were weaker and hungrier each day. The two armies were setting fire to each other's crops, while fishermen often returned to shore without a catch.

Marama's baskets and stone implements occupied a special place in the holds. Alongside of them lay Mohani's rongorongo tablets; the mariners' tools—stone ax, hammers, adze and chisels; fishing tackle—hooks, sinkers, handlines and nets of mulberry; weapons—three spears and three knives of obsidian. The craft was shipshape, well stocked but not overloaded. "Children of the sea-roads sail lightly," Te Rahai said, admiring the sleek vessel.

He summoned people to the harbor. Looking like a toy boat against a sea that stretched to the horizon, the ship rested on the sand, gleaming in sunlight. Every woman and child, every man not engaged in war appeared at the appointed time.

Te Rahai stood with his grandson on the beach. Miru observed the *reimiro,* a white amulet shaped like a canoe, hung around the sailor's wrinkled neck. Except for the growling of their bellies the crowd was silent.

In his arms Te Rahai cradled a ceremonial paddle whose likeness marked his body. The top of the wooden *ao* flared gracefully into a rounded image of the sea god: Tangaroa's wondrous face with his slender nose, engraved forehead, arched brows and round eyes, the whites carved of whaletooth and the pupils of blackest obsidian.

"Miru," the old pilot said, "this paddle, *Te Roku-o-witi,* has been used by mariners since the time of our first king." Ia's son knew the *ao* from songs and stories he had heard as a boy, when he had also seen it on his grandfather's twin-hulled ship. With reverence Te Rahai placed the paddle in Miru's hands. "I entrust it to your keeping. You're now a man of boats."

The *ao* was smooth and warm and alive in Miru's palms. He imagined it cutting through the water with spray flying from its blades. He had never felt such balance nor seen such beauty in a manmade thing. Moving through its fine-grained wood he sensed the cunning of the seamen who had sculpted *Te Roku-o-witi.* It would take him time to realize that he was a man of boats, like his grandfather and the two mariners, who had also manned the *ao* in their time.

"Miru!" Te Rahai called, "this paddle will aid and protect you on the voyage. It holds mana. Care for it in my name and for all our people."

The crowd broke into song, accompanied by women shaking seashells and men dancing on percussion plates of calabash:

Behold my paddle!
Behold my paddle, *Te Roku-o-witi!*
See how it flies and flashes,
it quivers like a bird's wing,
this paddle of mine.
Ah the outward lift and the dashing,
the quick thrust in and the backward sweep,
the swishing, the swirling eddies,
the foaming white wake, the spray
that flies from my paddle!

With the *ao* in his arms, dreaming of Kenetéa, his father and distant islands, the captain of the crew slept fitfully that night. In her slumber Renga Roiti saw Koro too, as well as schools of fish and flocks of her spirit birds. Mohani lay on his back, sleepless, with his eyes opened wide.

Dawn broke serene and bright. For sister and brother it was the day of days. Standing at the door of the great-house, with tears moistening their eyes, they said farewell to Ia and their uncle Ihu, saddened that their father was not there. Mohani wept as he remembered his parents and sister.

Renghi consoled the boy. "Our adventure begins today," she told him. "Tonight you'll already be singing songs of starpaths." The dawn of a smile fleeted over Mohani's lips.

Miru slung the great *ao* on one shoulder, his cloak on the other and strode away, looking like a man. Holding her head high, Renga Roiti walked at his side, no longer a girl, almost a woman. Mohani followed, shorter and lighter, still a child. The three crossed the square. Behind them straggled old Te Rahai.

A larger crowd waited on the beach. Above them Nuku, the king's elder son, stood on a platform. That mountain of a man towered over his bodyguard of red-clad Raa warriors. His broad trunk had offered a full field for the tattooer's craft: a volcano spouted lava up his chest and throat, over his neck and shoulders, while a second summit, bigger than the first, spewed fire and molten rock up his back, spiraling to a sky filled with black smoke and clouds.

Nuku's brother Kaimokoi waited behind him. Figures of spreading trees covered his lithe, sinewy torso. As he saluted the king's two sons, Miru recalled the day he had saved Kaimokoi's life in heavy surf, when they were boys and the clans lived in peace.

Attired in yellow, a phalanx of Tuu soldiers faced the Raas. They too were dressed for combat. At their front stood Engo, chief warlord of the tribe. His dark hair hung in braids from his skull to his shoulders, like the arms of an octopus, Miru thought. Three tattoos of sharks adorned his chest—one swimming underwater, another slicing the surface with a fin, a third rolling its body and opening its mouth to strike.

Koro's children and Mohani approached the platform. They appeared small and bare by those ranks of armed warriors.

Nuku raised a spear. "My father has declared a brief truce," he announced, "and has given us safe conduct to the coast." The soldier's throaty voice grated on Miru's ears. "The king wants this boat to sail with the colors of both tribes under his rule, Raas and Tuus." Turning to his troops, the prince ordered: "Hang the masts, decks, double stern and bows with streamers of red and yellow pandanus." They know nothing about ships, Miru thought, yet they want to decorate our canoe.

Kaimokoi addressed the sailors: "Make your journey in the name of Makemake, god of the air and soil, and Tangaroa, lord of fish and the sea." Startled to hear an invocation of the rival deities, people murmured. Miru remembered how Kenetéa had asked him to travel in the name of the two gods.

Strong men, home from the wars to attend the launching, placed wooden rollers beneath the ship's hulls. Amidst shouting, cheering and singing they pushed the two-masted canoe, slowly at first then faster, finally releasing it: the vessel sprang from their arms and alighted on the sea with a splash. Up to their chest in surf, those men rocked the twin hulls. The bows drank from the altar of gods. Finally a pair of those warriors mounted the boat, dropped its anchor-stone, dove off the side and returned to shore with the others.

Priests named the craft *Mahina-i-te-pua*, "Crescent wave that bursts into foam like a flower." Standing between Renga Roiti and Mohani on the shore, with the paddle cradled in his arms, Miru recalled that it had been the name of their first king's greatest ship. How could this tiny boat be worthy of the founder's canoe, he wondered, a vessel that was longer than a whale in the legends, tall as a tree, loaded to the gunnels with sailors, animals, crops and stores?

Suddenly the crowd felt the force of a wind blowing leaves in a gale: limping, a tall, muscular Raa soldier broke through the crowd. Miru saw a long white scar that snaked along the man's right leg, splitting the pattern of deep-blue, red and yellow tattoos that marked his body. His hair was black and lustrous like Kenetéa's. Recalling the blast of wind the soldier's enemies were supposed to feel when he stepped on the battlefield, he recognized Raunui, her father. He shuddered.

"Miru of the dolphins!" the warlord shouted.

That voice raised the hair on the arms of every man on the beach. Blood pounded in Miru's ears while Ihu's and Neira's warnings returned to his memory: "Be careful!" both had told him. He also reminded himself that this soldier had fathered Kenetéa and Mohani.

Miru paced forward, trembling and holding the *ao*. Dressed lightly for the journey, he looked slight and naked next to that warrior who bristled with armor and weapons: a shield strapped to one arm, in the other a great-shafted spear whose blade of obsidian flashed in the sea-light. Miru found it hard to take his eyes from the clouds of storm-blown leaves tattooed on Raunui's shoulders, or from the images of war clubs, crowned with human heads on the man's limbs. The soldier wore a brilliant red cloak and a reed helmet crowned with feathers.

The crowd closed around the two men, forming a circle on the sand.

"You've broken the taboos!" the warlord screamed at Miru, his nostrils flaring. "You've touched my daughter! You've spoken to my wife, trespassed on my people's territory and crossed the threshold of my great-house! Now you've kidnapped my son. I'm here to take him back."

As Raunui spoke, Mohani's eyes blinked in the sunlight. The boy seemed perplexed, looking first at his father, then Miru. Waves lapped on the shore.

Staring at the face of Makemake, the big-eyed god tattooed on the warrior's chest, Miru choked. "Raunui," he stammered, "look at our canoe." With his eyes set on his opponent, Kenetéa's father did not turn his head toward the ship. "It's about to embark on a quest that could save our island," Miru added, recovering poise, "and your son is part of our crew."

"He shall not leave Vaitéa," the man asserted.

"He shall," Nuku intervened, stepping forth and blocking Raunui with a lance. Miru noticed the prince's hands, his fingers like plump bananas where they grasped the weapon. His troops also lifted their spears. "My brother-in-arms," Nuku told the man, "your son shall go because the ship must have at least one of our tribesmen on board."

Kaimokoi addressed Raunui in turn: "That's the king's desire. Whatever the canoe finds on its voyage shall be split between the tribes." Miru and his sister looked at each other, astonished that the Raas would claim a part of the venture's rewards before it had begun. Glancing at Mohani, who stood between them, both sighed, aware that they could not dispute with their rivals here, that they must launch their canoe.

Hemmed in by soldiers from his tribe, Raunui did not move or speak. That warrior glowered at Miru. Meanwhile Mohani admired his father with wide-open eyes.

Kaimokoi faced the crewmen: "Go in the name of the two gods," he pronounced in a resonant voice. Stepping closer, the king's younger son looked deeply into Miru's his eyes and whispered, "You can count on my support when you come back to Vaitéa. I haven't forgotten."

Miru returned the prince's gaze. Then he took Mohani's arm and led him to shore, feeling the tremors of the boy's slim frame and the sweat on his skin. Fearless, red-haired Renga Roiti came last, her braids bouncing on her shoulders. The crowd parted before those sailors.

The three walked into shallow water. Together they swam toward the boat that was anchored offshore, bobbing in swells. Miru climbed over the forked stern. He placed the *ao* upright on the deck, held out his arm and pulled the crew on board—first Mohani, followed by Renga Roiti.

Now at full weight the craft settled to its final trim. Miru and his sister exchanged looks. Between them Mohani gaped yearningly at Raunui. But he did not resist the arms that Ia's children extended to him, one on each side, as they searched the crowd for their own father. They did not see Koro and missed him sorely.

Surrounded by spearmen on the beach, Raunui glared at the captain. "We'll care for your son," Miru said under his breath, remembering his promise to lonely Neira.

Singers chanted:

> The canoe is light,
> the pandanus streamers flutter,
> the prow is ready to leap like a dolphin,
> O *Mahina-i-te-pua*, fly!

Miru hauled up the anchor-stone and secured it to the deck. "Bring out the sails!" he shouted to his crew. They unrolled stiff folds of tapa with a crackling sound that made his heart race. Wishing that he could be on that vessel too, Te Rahai watched from the shore, praying for his grandchildren, Mohani and the canoe.

Miru clasped the rudder. The two children plied their paddles, one on each hull; they did not have the strength to propel their ship beyond the breakers. The captain gave his sister the helm while he took *Te Roku-o-witi* in his hands.

He made a few strokes with the *ao*: the boat skimmed over a cresting wave, a breeze filled the sails, and the twin keels cut through the water. White foam flew back from the bows in a double arc. The people watched as the craft moved ahead of its churning wake. Some believed it was an unlucky omen that the crew had not been able to drive their boat beyond the surf without Miru's help.

"Stories say our first king had more than thirty oarsmen," one old sailor said to another on the beach. "Miru has two—one's a girl and the boy's weaker than a girl."

"He's breaking all the taboos," the other man remarked. "Who ever heard of children for the crew of a longboat? A girl on a twin-hulled canoe? How can they hope to reach another island and come back to Vaitéa?"

"We'll never see that ship again."

Miru looked at the shore for the last time, turned and stared out to sea. Neither the crowd on the sand nor Renga Roiti and Mohani, whose eyes were fixed on the horizon, saw the captain's face streaming with salt tears.

From songs and stories he knew they should run with the southeast trades: Miru sailed to the west, the tack from which the people's first king had reached Vaitéa. The boat sliced through the sea with her double prow, sprayed foam and plunged into swells. Whether the wind puffed high or low the vessel caught it, playful as a child. Dolphins raced ahead of the bows.

Swift-footed Renga Roiti moved like a lizard on board, scrambling to obey Miru's orders. She trimmed sails to just the right slant while her brother held their course. Mohani, always a step behind, learned by imitating the girl, storing every detail in his memory. Some primeval thing out of their people's ocean-wandering past was alive in them.

At first the crew sailed by day and slept at night. One steered; another worked the sails and kept watch in the dark; the third rested. If the sea was choppy, both Renga Roiti and Mohani maneuvered the sheets, one on each hull, while Miru kept the tiller firm.

Before long it was too hot to travel during the day. The crew reversed shifts. They could also hold a better tack by following starpaths invoked by Mohani at night. With a knife the boy notched a daily mark on a wooden rongorongo tablet, the ship's log, which he had tethered to a mast-mooring.

Constellations washed into the sea, new stars rose and fell. Little Mohani identified some of them from tales told by his grandfather, the singer of tales, schooled in knowledge of the past. But those stories did not tell of sailing to another island and returning to Vaitéa; nobody had done that.

On the twelfth day the winds abated. The ocean's skin turned smooth. As their vessel floated in the calm, Renga Roiti and Mohani passed their days swimming, splashing and diving. But Miru allowed only one of them in the sea at a time. He stayed on board, preferring to wash himself when it rained. How much he had changed since undertaking Marama's mission.

The crew mocked their leader. "Who ever heard of a leaping dolphin who won't swim!" Mohani called one afternoon, treading water off the beam. Renga Roiti laughed from the boat's shelter.

"Nobody," Miru muttered, wishing he could be a child like them.

"Freckle-face!" Mohani piped. Miru saw the boy's mouth remain barely open—like Kenetéa's when she finished speaking—wet with seawater. He has ten summers, the captain thought, with a whole life ahead, shining on his lips.

In the still waters sea moss began to grow on the ship's bottom, attracting tiny fish who fed on the hulls and keels. The small fry and waste from the three friends' bodies drew larger fish and birds. Soon great-sharks surrounded the canoe. The pilot had already ordered Renga Roiti and Mohani to stop swimming, to keep their hands and feet out of the water. All day the crew watched the sharks' white, curved fins cutting the waveless sea around them. At night they listened to those sleek bodies banging and scraping against the hulls and keels. They could also hear flying fish flee the sharks: the quick beating of their wings as they rose above the water, their hissing flight, the soft splash when they glided back into the slippery path of death.

It turned hotter as the sun stood straight above them at midday. Sweat trickled down their backs. Mohani's eyes squinted in the light. Miru and Renga Roiti saw phantom islands on the horizon, dissolving then reappearing. They were in the calm where sailors can lose their minds.

On the fifteenth day Miru was asleep in the shelter while the other two tended *Mahina-i-te-pua*. Mohani tripped and fell between the hulls. In a flash Renga Roiti was over him, yelling and holding out a hand for the boy to grasp. He caught her wrist, but she did not have the brawn to pull him on board.

"Miru!" Renghi screamed as she saw two great-sharks homing on the child. One of them rolled on its side to strike, hit Mohani's thigh, shook its pointed head to tear off the flesh and dove away. Kenetéa's brother squealed like a bird while the water clouded with blood.

When Miru came running with the *ao* in his hands, the second shark had already thrust at the boy's bloody leg. The pilot smacked it on the head with *Te Roku-o-witi*, and the stunned creature sank into the depths. Miru pulled Mohani from the water. A red slick pooled on the surface where more great-sharks gathered. That blood is Kenetéa's too, the captain reminded himself.

The teeth had sliced two half-moons into Mohani's left thigh, exposing muscles, bone and tendons. He also had bruises where the sharks' coarse bodies had rubbed against his torso and limbs. To stanch the bleeding Miru tied a cord of braided hibiscus above the bites. Next he cleaned them with strips of tapa soaked in saltwater. Weeping, Renga Roiti covered her eyes.

Miru carried Mohani to the shade of the deckhouse. The child's body twitched. Brother and sister took shifts caring for their friend, washing his wounds, keeping him warm under folded sails.

When Miru attended the boy in the morning, Mohani still had not returned to the light. The child slept, breathing fast, his dark hair falling over his brow. How could the captain fail to recall Kenetéa? Miru remembered Mohani's parents and his promise to bring their son home to Vaitéa. Just then the boy's head tilted to one side, and his eyelids fluttered. Miru sensed how fond he had become of Mohani—their sea swallow, their mulberry shoot.

When the shock of the attack wore off, the child felt more pain. He moaned and cried for his mother, his father, Kenetéa. From dawn to death-light he sobbed.

Renga Roiti tried to comfort the boy. "Don't worry, little brother," she told him, caressing his face. "We'll make you better."

For days Mohani was feverish, and his body trembled. Writhing in agony one morning, he rolled out of the shelter and dropped over the side into the becalmed sea. Miru dove behind him, seized the child and raised his small body to the gunnels; swift Renga Roiti arrived to finish pulling Mohani on board. Before the great-sharks could strike him, the pilot clambered onto the boat.

The only way to make the boy safe was to strap him to the deckhouse. Fighting to free himself, Mohani squirmed like a fish, making the ropes dig deeper into his flesh. It saddened Miru and Renga Roiti to see their friend fettered like a prisoner.

The rain catchers and calabashes were almost empty of sweet water. The leader and his sister left the last drops for Mohani. Their mouths were dry, their backs burned, blistered and peeled, burned again. The canoe lulled on the waste of water. With his knife Miru marked the days on Mohani's rongorongo tablet, cursing the old witch for sending them on a wild quest.

The following afternoon it rained, wind stirred, and water seemed to blossom around the ship. Miru said a prayer of thanks to Tangaroa and Makemake. Their boat had crossed the dead waters.

Miru and Renga Roiti rigged the sails. While he took the helm, she jumped back and forth between the hulls, attempting to perform the work of two. Then he gave her the tiller and payed out the sheets of tapa cloth.

She did not have the strength to hold their course in the breeze. Miru returned to the steering paddle, disheartened, knowing their craft required a third crewman, however young and weak. The sails flapped while their vessel drifted on the sea.

Trying to navigage in the rising winds while they also watched over the boy, Miru and his sister worked without sleep. They scarcely had time to eat the little food that was left in the holds.

One afternoon the child told Renga Roiti that he felt hungry. After she had fed him the last pieces of smoked shark meat, she hurried to tell her brother, who was fighting to stay alert at the helm. The captain sighed with relief. He told Renghi to untie the cords that bound Mohani to the deckhouse.

The boy asked Miru for the rongorongos. With the wooden tablets in his arms he chanted verses. By evening he was reciting starsongs and notching the new day on his tablet.

Mohani observed Miru's sunburnt skin. "Your face doesn't look like a hill of ants anymore," he said. "It's all brown."

Knowing the child was well, Miru rejoiced. "And you've lost so much weight that your ears look bigger," he told Mohani, poking the boy's head. "If our sails rip and tear in a storm, we'll tie you to the mast and your ears will catch the wind."

The corners of the child's lips curled upward. It was not his former smile; peering into the far side of death had changed him forever. But soon he could get to his feet and hobble around the decks. By the twenty-seventh day Mohani could sit at the rudder when the sheets were lowered. He was still too feeble to stand a course in a good wind or breeze.

The season of foul weather was close. The boat passed through a squall and shipped water. While Miru stayed at the helm, his sister and Mohani bailed the decks. They close-hauled the sails, and their craft beat into the wind's teeth, made an abrupt tack and flew like a bird again.

The next day was calmer. Miru noticed Renga Roiti dawdling about the canoe. "Tell me," he said.

She squatted next to him at the helm. Miru looked into her face; Renghi's green eyes always reminded him of their mother's. They were his eyes too.

"Brother," she asked, "do you remember what our uncle told you in the longroom? That you shouldn't risk your life?"

"Yes."

"When you jumped in to save Mohani from the sharks, did you recall Ihu's words?"

"There wasn't time."

"If anything happened to you . . . he and I wouldn't last, would we?"

"No. And without Mohani, you and I wouldn't last long either. Renghi, it takes three of us to manage in a high wind. We also need Mohani for his starsongs that keep us on course at night. No matter how frail he is, we can't do without him. Together we make up a crew."

Red-haired Renga Roiti stared at the horizon. "There's something else," she said. Miru waited for his sister to explain. "My birds have gone," she told him.

"I know. Why?"

"We must be too far from land. They can't reach us—not even the strongest fliers like terns and swallows. How I miss them!"

Miru placed one arm around Renghi's small shoulder. Their old rift, born when he and Kenetéa had left his sister and their friends for love, was vanishing on the sea. Meanwhile he still dreamed of the thin-ankled girl.

On the thirty-third day the sky dawned cloudy as a pearl. A surge rose, and their craft rolled on the swells. The sea turned gray, the planks of great-palm creaked, ropes slapped in the mounting wind. Tears of the rain-god Hiro poured from black thunderheads. Pressing *Te Roku-o-witi* to the deck with his feet, Miru clutched the tiller in both hands. Their little boat was about to face its first storm.

He ordered his crew to lower the sheets and twin masts. Renga Roiti and Mohani struggled with the tackle; they could not do the job alone. Yelling above the wind, Miru commanded the boy to sit at the rudder while he and his sister secured the masts, rigging and sails; they also tied the empty chicken cages and brimming rain catchers to the deck. But Mohani could not hold the steering paddle steady. The ship veered one way, then another until the pilot returned to the helm. Through slanting rain Miru watched Mohani lurch to the gunnels and vomit over the beam. The boy retched, gagged, cried and vomited more.

The wind gusted harder as they neared the storm's heart. Their canoe strained, listed, yawed and pitched. In the dying light Miru saw Renga

Roiti clinging to one of the masts that lay flat on the deck. Where was the boy?

"Mohani!" he called in the howling air.

Renga Roiti tried to shout something; her voice was muffled by the roar of sea and wind. For a moment she let go of the mast with one hand to point below. The child must have fled, Miru understood, seeking refuge in the holds. The wind changed and blew Renghi across the deck. She tumbled, hit the mooring and hugged it with both arms.

The tempest raged in the darkness. Soaked in rain, beaten by the gale, brother and his sister clung to their ship while Mohani cowered below. The sharp salt of sea spray ran down Miru's cheeks, down the lines of his nose, onto his lips. The taste of Kenetéa's mouth returned to his tongue.

Before daybreak the wind eased. The children of Ia's milk looked at each other through gray drizzle. Their boat had weathered a storm.

Miru stayed at the helm while Renga Roiti bailed water. When the ocean's skin had stretched smoother, she took the steering paddle. He raced from one side of the ship to the other, raising the double masts, hoisting sails and tightening the cordage. Their canoe floundered, running in circles.

At dusk Mohani came topside. The child's skin was paler than the folds of tapa cloth that were flailing in the breeze. Averting his eyes from Miru, he skulked toward Renghi. She and the boy bailed decks and holds through the night.

In the morning the sun rose above the world, filling the crew with hope. Renga Roiti and Mohani set the sails. With Miru at the tiller the craft found her course again.

Their rain catchers had filled with saltwater, and their provisions were soaked, above decks and below. To chum for fish they used the spoiled food. They had to eat their catch raw from the handlines: all the sand in the firebox—the only place to cook—had been washed overboard.

For days Hiro did not shed his tears. The sailors' throats were parched. Their bodies grew weary.

When she spotted a sooty tern flying over the water one morning, Renga Roiti cried out with joy. In the late afternoon a pair of sea swallows wheeled around the vessel and alighted on the bows. Those birds looked tired, pummeled by winds and rain.

Miru looked at the swallows, their tiny bodies and delicate wings, amazed that they had survived the storm. They're like Renghi and the boy, he said to himself—small and weak on a vast ocean with waves and wind above, dark currents below. Like *Mahina-i-te-pua*, he thought.

With the seabirds for company Renga Roiti became herself once more. She spoke or sang to them as they perched on the ship's double bows and sterns. By the forty-fifth day she recognized the first homing birds—sooty terns that must have been flying out from land at dawn to feed, back in the evening to roost. She pointed to one that was skimming the water, dipping its head and plucking squid or shiny fish from the sea. At nightfall the captain aligned their boat's northwest tack to the terns' flight. Then Mohani tracked stars, and Miru righted their course.

Kenetéa's brother felt useful again, knowing the others depended on him to sing their ancestors' songs, to navigate by constellations. Mohani ceased shifting his eyes from Miru. But he did not seem to be the same boy who had embarked from Vaitéa. Distance, sharks and the storm had stolen his childhood.

The crew kept their new starpath at night and followed the terns in the mornings. On the fifty-third day a piece of sandalwood bark floated across the bows. Singing and jumping, Renga Roiti cried, "My spirit tree!" She dangled over the bowsprit, almost fell into the sea, laughing, reached, snatched the flotsam in her hand. She kissed the soggy bark. Renghi rubbed it on her limbs with their tattoos of sandalwood trees.

Three days afterward, in the morning, with his hand on the helm, the pilot detected faint land currents. Later he observed banks of clouds that were piling up on the horizon ahead. Miru recalled his grandfather's tips about these signs of nearby land.

Above the bows and true on bearing, it appeared in the early afternoon. With two tall peaks soaring through clouds, an island reared from the ocean before them, larger than anything they could have dreamed. The crew reveled, all three embracing. Miru and Renga Roiti hopped up and down, while Mohani bounded on the decks.

The island's summits reminded Miru of a sleeping woman's breasts. Already he could tell that this island was higher, longer and greener than Vaitéa. In silence he and his crew stared at it.

As the sailors drew closer, sandy white beaches dazzled their eyes. Thick groves of trees came down to the shore. Miru's heart leaped; could all of Marama's trees grow there?

They found no inlets or harbors. Yet the sea was calm, without the breakers that encircled most of Vaitéa. The island must be ringed by a reef, Mohani told them, using a word he had heard in ancient legends. Soon they learned that Kenetéa's brother was right: waves broke in a line of foam around the coast, separating the deep bluewater from light-green lagoons. Mohani recited a song that sung of red coral, the ocean's teeth, and how it had gnawed, bitten and destroyed the keels of their ancestors' boats.

Staying well out to sea now, the leader and his crew ranged the shore in search of a landing place. On the leeward side of the island they found a gap in the ring of breakers, only a little wider than their ship's beam, forming a passage into a lagoon. From the bows Renga Roiti and Mohani watched for the reef, calling "Left!" or "Right!" as the captain made quick adjustments of the tiller. With a surge that made their stomachs flip, they shot through the channel; it reminded Miru of sliding a big wave on Vaitéa. The canoe stuck briefly, rasping, scraping over the red coral, freed itself and glided onto the face of the lagoon. They had never seen water so smooth, green and clear down to the sandy bottom.

Miru leaped over the side and dove beneath the boat to check for damage. Surrounded by schools of iridescent fish, he saw where the ocean's teeth had chewed the bottom—both hulls and keels. He surfaced, scrambled on board, dashed to one of the holds, fell to his knees and found a spot where the craft was leaking. He sped to the other side and found more slits in the plank boards, seeping water.

The pilot ordered his crew to drop sails. Their canoe shipped more water, faster now, listing to starboard. With Miru manning the *ao*, the others at their oars, they paddled hard. Just before it could sink into the lagoon, the vessel's bows eased onto the pale sand.

Chapter 7

Ragi

After embarking from Vaitéa, at the end of the world, two children and a young man had sailed for fifty-five days, enduring weather, sharks and doldrums to discover an island on the road of winds. They had made landfall.

When Miru and Renga Roiti hurtled onto the sand, their knees buckled. Both regained their footing and helped Mohani over the gunnels. The three friends hugged. Renghi leaped while Kenetéa's brother tried to jump, wincing in pain as he landed on his scarred leg. For his part the captain studied their canoe, beached on its side, thrashed by storms, gouged by coral; it could not make a return voyage. He knew more than the others what this would mean for their mission. But for now Miru was relieved to be on land.

The sailors were too fatigued to push their waterlogged vessel beyond the beach. With the crew at his side Miru said a prayer of thanksgiving. "*Ma Makemake, ma Tangaroa,*" he intoned, recollecting Kenetéa's words. He raised the *ao* above his head and drove its pointed blade into the sand between the ship's bows, where *Te Roku-o-witi* wobbled. He, Renga Roiti and the boy unstepped the masts, lowered the sails, furled and stashed them in the hold. Then they turned their backs on the boat and struck inland. The air was fragrant around them.

Like children in a race the three fought to stay ahead of each other. Mohani stumbled and could not keep up. Renga Roiti and Miru let him take the lead. Moist and cool under their feet, dense grass covered the earth. Miru recalled when he had wandered in fields and shadowy forests with Kenetéa. How he would have wanted her to be there now, to explore this island in freedom, without parents, forbidden places or tribes at war!

Swaying in the wind, treetops towered over them. Brother, sister and Mohani caressed and fondled the trunks—larger than the hulls of their canoe—the branches and leaves. Some of those trees they had seen at home; others were unknown to them. The scenery awed the three crewmen. Each object looked like something in a dream.

The green island seemed made for them alone. Monkeys in the trees, birds of the shore and air showed no fright of the new beings in their midst. The visitors saw no signs of humans.

They climbed hills that were lush with grass, bushes and groves of trees. Flowers grew so thickly that their blossoms jostled each other in the breeze. The three ran down valleys where streams and rivers rushed, limpid as the sky where they pooled. The travelers dove into the freshwater. They drank it—the sweetest they had tasted—splashed each other and washed the caked sea salt from their skin. They peed on the rich earth. They picked ripe berries, gobbling them as they ran in the fields, spitting the half-chewed pulp on the ground.

Faster than they had ever seen on Vaitéa, night closed its dark wings over the island. They camped by a stream that flowed through a grove of sandalwood. Miru was content to find the first of Marama's trees, while Renghi thrilled to be sheltered by one of her spirit creatures. The exhausted sailors lay down to rest. With their heads still rocking from the sea, they slept to the music of running water.

At dawn they awoke to a new world. Birds were watching them from the ground or hovering over them. The wings, beaks, bodies and tails of those creatures had colors that did not exist in the speech of Tuas and Raas. But keen-witted Renga Roiti knew their language of chirps and songs. She spoke to them in soft coos. Between her calls she whispered, "This one may be a heron, that one an owl, those are parrots." They were the birds that used to live on Vaitéa.

"Could this be the island of our ancestors?" Renghi asked the others.

"No—it doesn't match our songs and stories," Mohani replied. "And where are the people and their animals? According to the legends, when our founders sailed from the first homeland they left women, men, children, dogs, pigs and hens behind." Miru and Renga Roiti looked at one another, thinking that Mohani sounded older than a boy of ten. In each other's eyes the brother and sister saw that the journey had aged them too.

Their ship lay where they had beached it, keeled to one side, the *ao* fixed in the sand between the tipped bows. For many nights the crew slept on the sea-torn craft. When spring storms began to buffet the coast, they removed their canoe's anchor-stone so that they could drag the vessel out of harm's way, farther up the beach.

The three moved to a cavern on a hill, where they had a view of the boat and could keep their stores dry. Miru pulled *Te Roku-o-witi* from the sand. He bore it to the cave. The *ao* would be the focus of their hearth.

The crew explored the island. At the head of valleys they found cascades glistening in the sunlight. Mohani had not heard of them in stories, so they invented their own name—"sky-rivers." Unfamiliar constellations they called "night-blossoms." Iridescent shellfish were "rainbows of the sea." The friends also created words for new trees, plants, birds, fish, creeping and swarming things. Using the old language of their people, they called the island *Ragi*: paradise.

Speech could not tell the marvel of the place. It was enough to talk with looks and gestures; they spoke less and less to each other. They sensed the failure of words to convey what they were seeing with their eyes.

At first they explored the island together. But after living at such close quarters on their ship, the three sailors soon sought time alone. Each took to a different part of Ragi: the leader roamed distant forests, his sister followed birds inland or to the coast, the boy chanted songs to monkeys in the nearby woodlands.

Feeling the old desire that the sea had driven from his body, Miru dreamed of the wished-for girl, her slim legs and high, round breasts. In the mornings he woke with his own milk curdled on his groin. He wondered at the power of a love that could cross an ocean. Am I still a slave of my heart, he asked himself, recalling Marama's words. Miru also dreamt of his mother and father.

Renga Roiti's first blood flowed. On an island with only a boy and a young man for company, she entered womanhood without recognition or ritual. During her moon-days she fled the cave. For the first time she missed her homeland, the confinement room of her family's house where she would have been comforted by women who understood the changes in her body, who possessed the rope of wisdom.

Longing for his family, Mohani limped around the landfall. He lost his appetite and stopped bathing in the streams. The boy stank like a beast. His only task was to notch a new day on the rongorongo tablet each morning.

One day Miru came upon thickets of mulberry, hibiscus, sandalwood and toromiro trees. Wherever he searched, he could not find great-palms or coconuts. The first of those missing trees was a totem of Kenetéa's; the second, one of Mohani's. Knowing the boy would be distressed to learn the news, Miru decided to say nothing. He also imagined Téa's, Te Rahai's and the witch's sadness if the expedition returned without the palms and coconuts that provided lumber for ships and houses as well as oil, milk and meat for food. As though he were waking from a dream, Miru recalled the condition of their canoe, unfit to sail.

He nourished himself on wild foods. He picked fruits from trees, sliced them open with the blade of his knife, sucked their juices and devoured their pulp, remembering at times the day he had slit a stolen yam by his family's well. He ate bunches of bananas that reminded him of Nuku's fat fingers. Since the day of the launching, that mountain of a man, the older prince, had stuck in his memory along with Raunui.

One afternoon Miru entered a valley where venerable groves of sandalwood grew. A reef of clouds raced across the sky, lightning flashed, thunder boomed, and Hiro's tears poured. The island hummed and swayed in the storm. It was not the sound or movement of the earth or air or sea—it was all of them at once.

Miru sat on the soft earth beneath a large tree, recalling a night when the white-armed girl had taken his arm and led him to the coast. She had stepped into the moonlit surf ahead of him. The lovers did not dive into the deep water, float on their backs or stare at the ocean of stars as they had done many times before. She stroked back to shore, and Miru followed her.

Without speaking a word Kenetéa had guided him to Mataveri, the plain where they could watch the rituals, concealed behind bushes. Side by side they observed Raa priests shuddering in rapture, men and women writhing in the dust, the manbird screaming in triumph as he held the sacred egg aloft, borne on a litter by his followers, who shouted insults against Miru's people.

When the crowd had left, he and Kenetéa squatted on the ground. In the dark she daubed the earth with her blood.

"Last night I started my moon-days," she told Miru. "Tonight I've bled in the cove where we swam. Here I've reddened the soil." Kenetéa paused. Crickets chirped in the grass. "My blood is for peace—for us and our tribes. We're all different and all one, like the earth and sea."

Miru stirred from his reverie. Hiro's tears were already passing from the valley. The green island ceased rolling in the storm; sun shone through the tops of the sandalwood trees. Vapor rose from the forest floor and wrapped Miru in a veil of fog. Thinking of Téa still, he moved slowly forward.

He came to a clearing where rays of sunlight slanted through the mist. Miru raised his eyes and beheld a vast, arching tree, wider than a whale and taller than a hill, whose crown was circled in clouds. Every branch, twig and leaf sparkled with rain. The tree looked like a giant waking from sleep, stretching its arms where birds darted in and out of the foliage, banking, diving and trilling songs. That whole creature thrummed with life.

Walking on tiptoes, as if he were approaching a slumbering god, Miru stepped closer. Then he lost his shyness and felt drawn to the tree like the birds in its branches, the ants swarming on its bark, the crawling things around its roots. He extended one arm toward the trunk, broader than the beam of the twin-hulled canoe. Like the skin of an animal it was alive to his touch. Miru stroked and caressed the grooved bark. He tried to embrace the tree, but his arms failed to gird its trunk. He dropped his hands, knelt and laid his head on a root, thicker than his thighs, where he fell asleep.

When he awoke, the mist had gone. The tree was rustling with more life. Insects buzzed, birds dove, fluttered and chirped around it. Thrusting back his head, Miru could view the whole creature now: he saw its top shining in the sun, towering into a sky as blue as the water beyond the island's reef. Some old branches, fat as tuna fish, were charred by lightning, but new limbs had sprouted from the blackened spots. Never had he seen a stronger, fuller or greater thing. Somehow the spreading tree reminded Miru of his father.

He watched the creature drink water from Ragi's earth and sky, swallow its air and light. He stayed under the tree's shelter, inhaling its breath, collecting the dark nuts that fell from its branches. Miru cracked them on the roots, peeled them and ate their flesh—whiter than bow-waves of the canoe.

Days rolled on like a dream. The moon rose and set, grew and waned. Spring came with fewer changes than on Vaitéa. Seasons were constant on that green island, each one almost the same as the one before it. Alone, without celebration, Miru turned sixteen. Meanwhile Renga Roiti and Mohani entered their eleventh summer.

Under the shadow of the spreading tree Miru felt a bliss he had not known since the days with Kenetéa. He spent his time in thought, in daydreams, remembrance and prayer. Sometimes Renga Roiti and Mohani came to mind; he missed them and regretted they could not see the island's heart. But now Miru needed to be alone. He must have been happy because he often wiggled his toes on the bed of fallen leaves. For the time being he had forgotten the ship's plight.

Miru began to hear voices in his sleep. They blended with the breeze, mere tremors of the air. "Miru!" they seemed to sing. When he would awake at dawn, he glimpsed forms fleeing through the shaded forests, tall figures, graceful as young women. Their feet barely touched the earth as they glided across the meadow where it met the trees. He could only catch sight of them by looking sideways; if he blinked, the visions disappeared. Miru remembered Marama's words about the beings who had lived on Vaitéa. In the presence of those spirits he felt secure, at peace. They guarded his solitude. Miru dwelled there deeply.

One morning he hunted for offshoots of the sheltering giant. He found them growing beyond its canopy. Some were saplings, others larger, many mature. None was half as big as the great tree in the clearing, the valley's center.

Time passed. The wind changed, and Miru caught a scent of saltwater. For the first time since landing on Ragi, he yearned for the ocean, altar of the world.

He left the valley. He traveled by day and slept in the foothills at night. On the third morning he saw the windward shore below him. Miru realized how much he had missed the place where land, sea and sky meet. He walked down to the white sand.

Dolphins clustered in the lagoon, swimming in a circle to keep the world in harmony. That day and others he swam to them. His totem brothers brushed against Miru with their sleek, smooth bodies.

In the afternoon he spotted the spirits again, flitting along the beach, floating through the groves that grew almost to the shoreline. Before he could discern their features, they were gone. All that remained was a palpitation in the air, a faint music of the trees, waves and wind, sighing his name.

Miru awakened one morning to a strange sound. He looked toward the ocean and saw what he could only have dreamed before. Chills ran through him: a fleet of longboats was plying beyond the reef, close enough for him to make out serried rows of paddles on each hull, spears that bristled on the decks. Oarsmen sang a deep-voiced chant in time to measured strokes that churned the water, cutting white paths on the sea. On his hands Miru counted the ships, on his feet when he ran out of fingers, with lines on the ground when he had used up all his toes.

The man-voices waned as the fleet grew smaller on the blue horizon. Those canoes were heading to the west. Where were they going, and from where did they come? Miru felt a sensation he had never known: those sailors were foreign yet familiar, much more like his own people than the spirits of the woods, fields and shore. He stopped to reflect: could I be the first man from Vaitéa to see inhabitants of another island?

Then Miru listened for the graceful spirits' voices. He did not hear them. Had they fled from the invaders as they had escaped the armies on Vaitéa?

He walked back toward the leeward coast. At death-light on the second day he arrived at the cavern, whose mouth was overgrown with bushes and vines. Except for *Te Roku-o-witi* at the hearth, the cave was empty.

Miru ran down to the coast where they had beached their ship. Stunned, he saw the rigging strewn on the pale sand, cut and ripped, the sails gashed with knives, masts chopped to splinters, the twin hulls and keels crushed, decks shattered. On the mutilated sterns and prows he observed piles of excrement reeking in the sun. Footprints surrounded the canoe. On the sand Miru saw tracks where longboats must have been dragged to shore and out to sea again.

His howl carried to Ragi's mountain-tops. Monkeys scampered to their caves, spiders scurried into their holes, birds frightened and flew away. Through the night Miru clawed his face, wept and writhed in the canoe's debris.

At dawn he hunted for Renga Roiti and the child. Around noon he heard a feeble voice. He followed it to a cavern on a hillside, where he found Mohani alone in the dark, cringing in a corner.

Kenetéa's brother told him that a boat had made landfall on the beach a few days ago. Its oarsmen had debarked and assaulted *Mahina-i-te-pua*. He had watched from the hill as those men battered the canoe with knives, axes, war clubs—even the ship's anchor-stone. Laughing and singing, the marauders had defecated on the double prows and sterns, Mohani said. They had scoured the area around the beach, found nothing, departed and joined a fleet of boats beyond the reef. They had sailed to the west, where those vessels dropped over the horizon.

Mohani had not seen Renga Roiti for thirty days now, he told the captain, each one scratched on his rongorongo tablet. The boy also revealed that he had started to repair the craft before the intruders' arrival, tired of waiting for the older members of the crew, eager to make the voyage home, to see his family.

Miru placed a hand on Mohani's arm, whose down was clotted with grime and sea salt. "We'll rebuild our ship together," he said, looking into the child's black eyes, "and sail her home." Miru's words sounded false to his own ears. He knew that he, his sister and Mohani lacked the skills to make their boat snug and seaworthy again, that they might be marooned on Ragi forever.

"How long will it take?" the boy inquired.

"If you help, we may leave by the end of summer." Ia's son coughed to avoid choking on his words.

"I cannot wait that long," Mohani moaned. Miru recalled when he had once said those words to Kenetéa. "Besides," the child added, "Te Rahai told us not to sail in the season of summer storms." Miru smiled to himself. Téa's brother was too smart to fool.

A bird passed overhead. "When will Renghi come back?" Mohani asked.

"Soon," Miru responded, hoping it was true.

In the morning they combed the island for Renga Roiti. They did not find her that day, the next or the following. They searched and searched. Without her presence the cave seemed empty and forlorn.

The pilot regretted ignoring his sister. He and Renghi had been so close as children! Their mother would raise one of her long, dark fingers, Miru remembered, saying proudly, "My son and daughter are like flesh and nail." He and Renga Roiti had done everything together: they spun tops and flew kites woven from bark cloth, made music by blowing blades of grass between their thumbs, ran naked on slopes and beaches, explored shadowy woods and valleys. As long as the tribes were at peace, he and his sister could cross the border to be with Raa children, who could also travel in Tuu lands. So they met the lovely girl whose parents only let her play at dusk or on cloudy days, Kenetéa, who followed them on excursions when she was free. Then something had changed. Suddenly every place on Vaitéa appeared different: never had Miru and Kenetéa seen the world look so fresh as when they were together, nor felt the warmth that rose like a soft flame in their chests. Soon they began to outrun Renga Roiti, mislead her and escape to more secluded retreats. With the cruel blindness of lovers they neglected the girl. Miru and Téa nursed a secret guilt for fooling her; it made those moments remorseful and delicious. They were not willing to share their new life with her, with their friends or anyone. They had found their own island.

Miru and the boy gave up the hunt for Renghi. When she returned, five days after their search, it was on her own. She had grown taller, her red hair hung below her shoulders, her hips were wider, and two buds had blossomed on her chest. Seeing her brother and Mohani gape at her, she blushed and lowered her eyes.

That evening Miru and the child told her how the sailors had scuttled their canoe. Renga Roiti sobbed through the night.

At dawn the three friends gathered around the hearth. Renghi's eyes were moist and bloodshot.

Mohani cleared his throat. "I forgot to tell you something about the strangers," he said, looking away from sister and brother.

"What?" Miru asked.

"They used the language of our ancestors."

"How do you know that?" Renga Roiti cried.

"I recognized words from old songs, poems and stories. Their voices were forceful—the sound traveled all the way to the hill where I was hiding." Still averting his eyes, the boy paused, recollecting. "Some of their

WIDE AS THE WIND

ships were loaded with fruit, lumber and other goods that I couldn't make out from a distance."

Miru understood that the longboats he had seen the other day, pulled by oarsmen and lined with spears, had been only a part of the travelers' fleet. From that night he, his sister and Mohani never spoke of the incident. It was part of their shameful secret; their canoe must have been ravaged by descendants of their own tribes, those who had stayed behind when their first king embarked on an expedition to find a new place to settle. The homeland of those people must be wasted like Vaitéa, the three suspected. Like the Tuus and Raas those sailors must also have drawn away from the world, lost their mana, fought each other, succumbed to men with bloody hands, eventually launched a voyage to seek food, trees and supplies that were scarce on their island. They had probably wrecked and defaced *Mahina-i-te-pua* because they did not want to divide Ragi's treasures with another people.

Miru wanted to follow his grandfather's advice, to wait out the weather, to allow the summer storms to pass before sailing. But his crew had turned sullen, moping about in the flyless heat. Renga Roiti missed Ia with her voice like lapping waves, her father, Te Rahai with his great calm, her uncle Ihu. Mohani pined for his parents and sister. And Miru longed to embrace his mother, to make peace with Koro, to see Te Rahai and the canoe-shaped amulet around his neck. Although he had surrendered hope of being with Kenetéa again, he still ached for her and dreamed of the little seeds at the center of her eyes.

If he and his crew lingered on the green island, Miru worried, they might grow stale and lose their mana, the strength they needed for the return. He came to a decision. It was as hard as the one he had made to receive Marama's call.

He walked to the shore where the boat lay on the sand. He saw cracks in the hulls that Mohani had tried to seal before the invaders had done their damage. Miru climbed on board and rummaged for the shipbuilders' tools. Deep in the holds he found them—the stone ax, hammers, adze, chisels—buried in rubble.

He led his sister and Mohani to the edge of the ancient groves. When they arrived, they saw where the intruders had axed many trees to stumps. The odor of fresh-cut wood hung in the air. Miru's eyes burst with tears.

Leaving Renghi and the boy behind him, he ran to the spot where he had found the great, arching tree. Miru sighed when he saw it rise out of the clearing. He consoled himself by thinking that it was too big for strangers to bring down. He prayed that it would grow in peace, unharmed by men.

Koro's son knew what he must do. In the presence of his sister and Mohani, he chose a pair of the spreading trees that survived in the groves. "*Ma Makemake, ma Tangaroa,*" he invoked, silently adding the spirits of the woods and shore to his prayer, "pardon us."

With pain in his heart Miru felled the two trees. Afterward he collapsed in exhaustion on the forest floor. He slept with Renga Roiti and the boy by his side.

At first light they began trimming one of the trees for masts. They cut and hollowed another for decks, keels and prowboards. Over the next three days the friends dragged the unfinished logs to the coast, where the longboat was beached like a sad, wounded whale. Miru would have liked to let the new heartwood cure for a month or more. But there was not time; the remade craft would never be as watertight as one framed with seasoned lumber. He also would have preferred to replace its old hulls, grated by the ocean's teeth, mauled by the raiders. But he and his crew did not possess the knowledge or experience to build a whole vessel the size of their canoe.

While the captain and his sister shaped the logs, Neira's son related stories about master shipbuilders of old. As Miru and Renga Roiti pieced the planks and bound them together, Mohani sang songs of the founder's journey to Vaitéa. With dried skins of stingrays caught in the lagoon, Ia's children sanded the new strips of wood as well as the lacerated keels and decks, the smashed prowboards, sternposts, deckhouse and firebox, while their little friend told legends about the hero kings. When they caulked and painted the twin hulls with moss, shell-lime and ochre, the child intoned starpaths he had learned from his grandfather. As Miru and Renghi braided hibiscus for ropes and rigging, Mohani recounted his ancestor-lines from the beginnings to the tribal wars. While they wove mulberry bark for sails, the boy recited poems about that tree, one of his totems. "The sheets made of my spirit brothers will catch winds and take us back to Vaitéa," he boasted.

Before brother and sister had completed their work, Mohani ran out of stories, songs and starpaths. The child started repeating what he had already sung or told. Miru believed that he and Renghi would go mad if the boy went on much longer.

Their canoe was as ready as the crew could make it. The masts leaned, the decks sagged, both hulls were crooked. Miru guessed the boat would sink in the first storm. Perhaps old Marama was right: he chose loves and voyages that were impossible. As he studied the ship, a wild thought flitted through his head: what if we forgo the inbound journey, what if we stay on Ragi? But when the captain recalled Mohani's and Renga Roiti's impatience to embark, when he evoked his family and Kenetéa, he abandoned the idea. Do not allow fear to turn your mind, he told himself.

He and his sister carried Marama's implements and her three baskets to the valley. There they harvested seeds, cut shoots and pulled choice saplings of the giant tree, hibiscus, mulberry, sandalwood and toromiro. Miru and Renga Roiti made trips back and forth from the woods to store them amidships, in the safest part of the hold. They set the life-giving seeds in one of Marama's waterproofed baskets. In another they placed the shoots, nestled in earth, wrapped in banana leaves. In the third basket they put the tender saplings, covered lightly in soil, bound at the roots by moist bark and tapa cloth.

For the last time Miru traveled to the sheltering tree. He clasped it, feeling that he was embracing his father too. Inside the trunk he sensed a great heart beating. He said goodbye to the tree and the spirits who resided in the groves.

The loading of the boat lasted a full day and night. The crew filled calabashes with rainwater, stocked the holds with their tools, sinkers, handlines and fishhooks, fruits, berries and nuts, plantain leaves to fuel the firepit.

While the others were asleep in the cavern, Renga Roiti slunk to the beach. In the dark she hung the craft's bows, sterns, masts and rigging with the faded red and yellow pandanus streamers from the outward sailing. The young woman also hid something in the hold.

The morning broke windy and bright. Bearing *Te Roku-o-witi* in his arms, Miru led his crew to shore, where they saw those banners fluttering in the breeze. He smiled for the first time since their canoe had been demolished.

He lifted the *ao* and drove its blade into the sand. Around it the three sailors formed a circle. Miru raised a prayer for a safe return. In silence he implored the gods and spirits to keep their ship's course away from storms and the fleet of warriors. The crew made offerings of fruit, fish, shells and flowers.

Miru pulled *Te Roku-o-witi*'s pointed tip from the sand. He, Renga Roiti and Mohani pushed the double stern; they could barely nudge the vessel into the green shallows of the lagoon. As they rocked it from side to side, the hulls drank from the altar of the world. The crew climbed on board.

There were no singers to chant songs and celebrate the launching, no women to shake seashells or men to dance on drums of calabash. Miru fondled the ceremonial *ao*. To the boat he whispered, "O *Mahina-i-te-pua*, fly!"

Chapter 8

Gates of the Sun

Tangaroa sent a boisterous wind that drove their craft across the green lagoon. Miru steered toward the opening in the coral, a mere hand's breadth wider than their canoe, where the red teeth had chewed the bottom on the day of landfall. This time their vessel skimmed over the reef, just grazing the twin hulls. It approached the line of breakers and shot through the channel onto the open sea.

Miru set a bearing to the southeast. The ship's bow waves foamed whiter than milk. As it drew away from the island, the sailors looked back, surveying the reef, lagoon, the beaches and two summits in the shape of a woman's breasts. That island has nourished me like a mother, Miru knew; made me grow and learn, showed me the graceful spirits and the spreading tree, taught me to be in the world with a quieter heart.

It was too hot to travel by day. When the sun shone, the friends huddled in the shade of the deckhouse with the sheets dropped and the steering paddle tied to its course. At night they voyaged on starpaths memorized by Mohani and woven into his verses.

For fifteen days their ship ran with the trades. The timbers groaned, the masts bowed, and the sheets blew taut in the wind. Seeking the morning sun, the boat followed the wake of the crews' ancestors. Miru remembered tales of the founder's canoe, loaded with people, animals and cargo, driven by tall sails and the arms of powerful oarsmen. Studying their little craft as it strained in the breeze, his sister and the child who made up its crew, he felt small and unprotected on the broad ocean, wide as the wind. What if the fleet of warships should spy *Mahina-i-te-pua*—the boat which the invaders believed they had scuttled for good, he wondered. Keep your head, Miru admonished himself: those warriors had rowed into the setting sun, not toward Vaitéa in the east.

Every afternoon they passed through Hiro's tears. The pilot knew those squalls could herald bigger storms. He allowed the showers to water his saplings and shoots. On calm days he and his sister also carried the plants on deck for light and air. Between shifts at the sails or helm they checked the seeds to be sure they were dry in the hold.

The wind rose one morning. By noon the seas were choppy, ruffled by wind and specked with whitecaps. By mid-afternoon the sun had disappeared. Birds screeched and flew out of sight. Whales, dolphins and sharks sounded to the depths.

Thunderclouds pursued the sailors from the west, towering to the sky's roof, outracing their boat. Rain fell so hard that it hurt the crew's naked skin. Salt spray stung their eyes. The wind howled, the sea turned black as obsidian, waves clawed at the hulls.

Only Miru perceived how hazardous the coming storm could be for a canoe cobbled together with unseasoned wood. His nostrils quivered. He brushed *Te Roku-o-witi* with one hand, pleading for its mana.

With a cord of braided hibiscus Miru secured the steering rudder to the deck. "Come here!" he called through the wind to Kenetéa's brother, who teetered to his side. "Hug the tiller as tight as you can, Mohani!"

The vessel heaved, yawed and shipped water on all sides. Renga Roiti helped Miru take down the sails. After unstepping the masts they knotted them to their moorings and carried the furled sheets below, both of them stumbling, leaning against the wind. As they moved toward the helm in driving sheets of rain, they could scarcely discern Mohani, who was clasping the tiller to keep himself from being thrown into the sea. Renghi and Miru could not see that the child was shaking, his eyes pouring tears, his hands bleeding where he gripped the rudder.

A high wave hit on the starboard and threw Renga Roiti to the deck. Miru leaped to her side, landed on one foot, slipped, fell and rolled across the wet planks. He crawled back to his sister, who was lying on her belly, arms splayed. When he turned her over, she glanced up at him. She made the fearless little girl's smile he had not seen since she had become a woman.

"Don't budge!" Miru told her. The ocean thundered through his words, and she could not hear them. "Forgive me for this, Renghi," he said, strapping her to the deck with cords of hibiscus. She looked up with resignation as he pulled tight and knotted them.

Miru tried to stand. The wind gusted and blew him down. He labored to rise to his feet and tottered aft, feeling his way by passing his hands along the gunnels. A roller broke on the port side and knocked him to the deck. Rather than expose himself once more, Miru waited for the boat's stern to plunge; then he slid down the plank boards, and his body smacked against the rear bulkhead.

He raised himself high enough to peer at the helm. He saw what he had dreaded: through the rain, surf and storm-wash he could no longer glimpse the boy by the rudder. "Mohani!" he cried. The shrieking wind drowned his voice. He spotted *Te Roku-o-witi* still lashed to the deck, within reach, covered in a foot of water. Miru extended his hand to touch it. Next he turned, knowing it was useless to search for Mohani where swells engulfed the twin-forked stern. In the growing darkness, through slashing rain, he could not tell where the canoe ended and where the sea began in the boiling spume. The child was gone.

Miru felt a hollow in his chest. He roared his pain to the winds. He prayed to Tangaroa that the boy's soul would spin free of his drowned body, that he would find his ancestors beyond the sun's gates. He thought of white-armed Kenetéa, her parents; how they would mourn Mohani. Miru recalled his promises to the child's mother and father. They would blame him, the leader, for their loss.

Miru remembered Mohani's eagerness to return home. How the boy had tried to repair their boat himself, before the raiders had despoiled it. How he had faced death on the outward journey, lost his childhood, almost become a man. Those memories made Miru weep.

Water was rising on the decks. He noticed a bailer lodged against the bulkhead, grabbed it, scooped and hurled water over the side with all his rage and sorrow for Mohani's death. The vessel pitched in the bows and skidded down one swell, mounted to the peak on a second, swayed at the top, plummeted into the trough when a wave like a hill crested and broke on the decks with a smash, tearing the tiller from its ropes and throwing it to sea, whirling the hulls around and sweeping Miru feet-first over the stern.

He grasped blindly with both hands: one missed while the other caught a loose cord tied to a mast-mooring. Miru strained to tug himself in, swallowing seawater, spitting, stretching to keep his face above the surge. He edged his chin over the stern by the great bird's double tail, where he fell flat into the water that flooded the decks. Miru choked as brine gushed into his mouth and nostrils. Clenching the rope in one hand, he looped it around his legs, knotting the loose end so that he was bound to the mooring. As long as the ship stayed afloat, he could prop himself up with arms and elbows, and his head would remain above water.

Miru recalled Marama's baskets below decks, filled with seeds, shoots and saplings. He imagined them being tossed around the holds, sloshing in bilge, washing out to sea, lost forever. He also remembered the great tree with its sheltering crown. While the storm beat the canoe with rollers like cliffs, blowing it off course, while the wind deafened his ears, Miru longed for that spreading creature, for the solid earth, the meadow and the spirits who dwelled on Ragi. He thought about his family too: Koro, strong as a tree; shining Ia with her voice like water; old Te Rahai, tall Ihu; the square in front of their house, the well where pigs used to scavenge, where dogs napped in the sun, chickens pecked the dirt, and smoke curled above the thatch of roofs.

With Miru lashed to the helm, rain, wind and waves thrashed the ship through the night. At dawn he was sure that he heard both hulls cracking at the keels. He prayed. This must be how a man dies at sea, he told himself. Or a woman: Miru could not see his sister's red hair nor hear her cries above the gale and seething water. If she survives, she'll die of grief when she learns about Mohani, he feared.

"Renghi!" he called. In the crashing waves and screaming wind he heard a faint reply: "Miru."

The third day of the storm came and went. Brother and sister grew weaker without sleep, food or water, each one tied to a different part of the craft, each invisible to the other. On the fourth afternoon the wind dropped. The rain slackened, and the sea swallowed the last whitecaps in the falling light.

Miru removed the cords from his legs, tried to stand, tumbled to the deck, rose and gripped a plank where the helm had been torn from its housing and swept to sea. With the other hand he groped for the *ao* in the death-light, felt it, unbound and placed it in the empty tiller's slot. He knotted it fast with ropes from the loose cordage. *Te Roku-o-witi* was now the steering paddle, the new helm, a makeshift rudder that would have to keep their boat on course.

"Renghi!" he cried out again in the dark. He heard no response. He crossed to the starboard hull where he had strung his sister to the deck.

He found her, looking up at him with immense, frightened eyes. When Miru kneeled and unstrapped her, Renga Roiti saw the affliction on her brother's face. At once she knew. She shook and wept, calling and keening, "Mohani! *Aûé!* Mohani!" Miru embraced her. He could not console Renghi, and their canoe drifted on the sea.

When streaks of light chased the darkness, sister and brother performed a rite, entrusting the child's soul to Tangaroa and Makemake. Mohani was the first son or daughter of their island to be mourned in the name of both gods. Many more would follow him beyond the sun's gates.

Miru and Renga Roiti squatted where the deckhouse had been shattered by the storm. Tears still fell from clouds that were racing across the sky.

"Mohani, our sea swallow," Renghi whimpered.

"Our mulberry shoot."

"Remember those little hands?" she asked.

"Those ears like wings."

"His starsongs. Can you sing them, Ru?" Renga Roiti herself was surprised by the nickname that slipped from her mouth.

Once Miru had recoiled when she pronounced that word—the name he loved to hear on Kenetéa's lips. But he was too weary now, too harrowed by Mohani's death, too far from Vaitéa to care. What did it matter if Renghi used his secret name if he would never see the bright-eyed girl again? Miru was certain their ship would not reach home.

"Do you think I should have tied Mohani to the helm?" he asked his sister.

Renga Roiti brushed Miru's cheeks with her water-shrunken fingers. "Even if you'd bound him to the steering paddle, he would've been washed away with the tiller. The storm ripped out the whole thing and threw it overboard."

In the spreading light Ia's children inspected the damage. The ruined deckhouse would no longer shield them from the heat. They would not be able to use the firebox, splintered by the storm, to cook or heat food. The two bows had been mangled by storm-waves. One stern had dropped its bird's tail, forcing the canoe to heel, to cut a crooked wake. But as far as brother and sister could tell, their longboat's hulls had not split at the keels.

Miru's dagger of obsidian, sheathed to his arm, was the only weapon that endured the storm. The rest—their other knives and three spears—like their stone tools, had disappeared. A single rongorongo tablet remained where Mohani had tethered it to a mast-mooring. In the warped, moist wood Miru notched the three days of the storm, recalling the child and feeling a pull on his heart.

He walked below decks. Bilge and spray had soddened their foodstuffs. Marama's baskets had been thrown around the holds; the waterproofing of banana bark had not kept their contents dry. The brine had swept away many seeds. Most of the shoots had died or vanished. All the saplings had lost the soil, bark and tapa cloth that swathed their roots; some had drunk too much saltwater to survive. Miru felt as though they were his own children—parts, limbs from his body—who had perished or were marked for death. Our mission has failed, he told himself.

When Miru returned above, Renga Roiti scrutinized him; she noticed the change in her brother's countenance. She handed him the rudder and descended to the hold, where she also observed the loss of shoots and seeds. Weeping, from a hidden spot she pulled a reed cage, one of those they had used to keep chickens on the outward passage.

She bore it to the deck and opened it. Renghi removed a pair of young swallows whose wings and tails had been soaked in seawater from the storm. Their eyes opened, blinked, shut and opened again in the sunlight.

She showed the birds to her brother at the helm. "At least something survived below," she said. Miru's dour expression hardly changed. "I hid these swallows the evening before we launched our boat," she confessed. Renga Roiti blushed as she stroked the birds' damp feathers, hummed, whispered and talked to them. "They remind me of him, our little sea swallow." She cried. Between her coos and sobs Miru heard Mohani's name over and over.

Renghi restored the birds and their cage to the hold and rejoined the captain. Taking her hand, he placed it on the new tiller: "*Te Roku-o-witi* will have to steer us," he told her. She felt privileged to grasp the *ao*, something a woman had never done. The thrill made her small frame tremble.

Red-haired Renga Roiti showed distress for Mohani's drowning, for the dead or damaged seeds, sprigs and shoots. But Miru had been mistaken: she did not die from sadness for their little friend. Nor did she lose hope. She never doubted that a ship piloted by her brother would reach port. Yet she was not the same person who had begun the homeward crossing with Mohani on board; neither was Miru. The boy's death had wounded both of Ia's children deeply.

The captain knew that their canoe required a crew of three in bad weather, even if the vessel had not been broken by the tempest. He and Renghi did not know the starsongs like Mohani, the chants whose verses had guided them on the outward voyage, whose words might have led them home. While his sister dozed at night, Miru thought the sails of their boat seemed to swell with pain. He wept.

Ia's son believed his decision to embark in late summer had been right. Yet he reproached himself for making it. He felt remorse for having lost those months in the shade of the sheltering tree, those days swimming and diving with dolphins on the coast, when he could have been refitting their canoe for the inbound journey. But if he had tried to repair the boat earlier, Miru realized, it would have been destroyed by those raiders in the end. He also fathomed that he had needed that time to be alone, to reflect on the mission, to stay in the valley, to know trees and the earth, to live by those spirits in the sacred groves.

For her part Renga Roiti regretted leaving Mohani in the cave while she lived among the birds. But those months were just as crucial to her as Miru's time to himself. Without the nights and days of thought, prayer and solitude, neither she nor her brother would have been prepared for the greater adventure of the return.

The canoe seemed empty without Mohani. High winds had stripped her colored banners. Like wraiths Miru and Renga Roiti walked over the decks. The boy's disappearance, the storm, the loss of seeds and shoots had crushed the mirth in their hearts.

The season brought cloudy skies and starless nights. For days on end they traveled without bearings, running before the wind.

One evening Renga Roiti told her brother, "We're alone. We don't have stars or birds to help us, Ru. How will we find the way?"

"We're lost, Renghi." He was too distraught to comfort her. Miru had forgotten what Te Rahai had taught him: a captain should never allow his crew to know the gravity of their plight.

Renga Roiti looked at him with wet eyes. "Brother, when I was living on the nesting grounds of Ragi, some of the older birds turned sick. I tried to care for them but they were too weak to eat, drink or fly. Soon they would just go off somewhere and disappear—I never saw them leave, never found their little bodies. They didn't leave a trace behind, not even a feather or two. It was as if they simply vanished in the soil or air."

"Why do you tell me this, Renghi?"

"It was a beautiful way to die."

For nine days they cruised on a following wind, gaining speed, passing through rain each afternoon. Miru knew their ship could not ride out a second storm.

When the sea's face smoothed its wrinkles, brother and sister's courage rose. They never thought they would delight to see the calms again. In the stillness of dead waters they were safe from tempests. But the heat grew, almost as dangerous as foul weather. With no deckhouse for refuge they could not escape the sun. In light or dark a sheen of perspiration coated their bodies. Their skin burned and blistered, bled, peeled, burned and blistered more.

Sultry nights followed scorching days. Miru and Renga Roiti had reached the strange waters where Hiro's tears do not fall, where the wind dies, sails luff, and mariners rot with heat. Their throats were parched, their tongues swollen, their lips cracked. To find relief they dipped bailers in the sea that was swirling with great-sharks, and they threw the water on their thirsty flesh. The salt dried and split the sores on their skin. They were tempted to dive into the flat ocean to cool themselves. The curved white fins around the boat made them desist; both remembered Mohani's accident on the outbound voyage.

They had lost their supply of fresh water in the storm. For days the rain god did not weep. Miru looked around, saying over and over, "So much water, none to drink," to Renghi, to himself or the air.

One evening some flying fish landed on the decks. Sister and brother ate them raw for their meat and moisture. Renga Roiti also fed the flesh to her young swallows. But those fish did not reappear in the quiet waters, devoured or driven away by the sharks that seemed to multiply around the ship.

Miru raved with thirst and fever. Stretching his hands between the mossy hulls, he scooped seawater and gulped it. Renga Roiti had such faith in him that she did the same. Both retched and vomited.

Their bellies had shrunk into knots, empty of food and water. Their bodies barely perspired; they licked the salty dew from their limbs. Through red eyes they scanned the horizon for islands or boats or miracles. An odd music rose from the sea.

"Do you hear it?" Miru asked.

"I've been hearing it for days. It must be what our grandfather warned us about—remember?"

"The song that sailors hear when they lose their minds."

Meanwhile the saplings withered. Miru attempted to spit on their leaves and soil to give them life. Before his saliva could reach the plants, it evaporated on his bloated tongue.

Most of the tender shoots died in the holds. Not one sprig or seed of sandalwood remained. Miru tried to imagine Marama's desolation if she ever learned, Renghi's too—he would not tell her for now. At any rate she was too feeble to leave the deck. If she discovered that her totem tree had been lost, he feared, his sister might despair. What would they do without her hope?

While she was asleep one morning, Miru dropped the dead seedlings overboard. As if they were children who had died, little brothers like Mohani, he said prayers for them while they bobbed on the slick surface.

Only a few saplings and seeds of hibiscus had been spared by the storm, along with some toromiro, mulberry and offshoots of the spreading tree. Those were the last remnants of Ragi's thick woods on the canoe.

Slowly and wearily the days passed. Miru and Renga Roiti had visions and dreams of dreams. They saw phantom islands looming ahead, always farther ahead, with rainbows arcing over mountain peaks. But there was no land or rain.

From watching and searching, their eyes looked remote, sunken deep in their sockets, seared by sunlight and the shimmering sea. Their arms and legs were thin as reeds. Miru's ribcage resembled a ship's skeleton. The curves of Renghi's young body had been worn down to her bones. Both guessed they had already perished and were sailing toward the sun's gates, two ghosts on a derelict canoe. Then they would touch their bleeding palms, burnt by ropes, wind and heat, knowing from the hurt that they must still be alive.

Their vessel bobbed like a toy on the sea. "Remember the tiny boat our grandfather whittled for us?" Renghi asked.

"Carved from toromiro wood."

"Remember how we sat with him on the paving stones at the harbor, where the old seamen told stories or slept in the sunlight?"

"Te Rahai was so proud of us."

"Remember how he called me his little bird?" Renga Roiti paused. "We were happy then, weren't we, Ru?"

He did not reply.

The pilot brooded on his family, wishing for their safety. For the first time Miru repented of leaving his island and his people. I might have been more useful as a soldier on Vaitéa, he thought, fighting at my father's side. Could Koro have been right, could he have been more farsighted than Mother and Ihu, more than Marama and Kenetéa, who all urged me to undertake this mad voyage?

The two sailors had eaten their last bits of food. They tightened the tapa belts around their waists. Even Renghi began to resign herself to death by starvation. She and her brother could have eaten the swallows and the final sprigs and shoots. But they would have preferred to succumb themselves; that would have been like consuming their own children.

One morning a breeze stirred. Soon Hiro wept. Miru and Renga Roiti looked up at the sky, opening their mouths, letting the drops fall onto their swollen tongues. The rising winds puffed against their sun-blistered faces. Brother and sister regarded each other, too exhausted to smile.

Miru brought the saplings onto the deck, where they could drink rain, light and air. Most had already shriveled in the darkness of the holds. A few revived in the fresh shower. Miru and Renghi fondled, nurtured and spoke to the seedlings.

Flying fish landed on their decks again at night. Ia's children gobbled the raw meat. Renga Roiti also fed the winged creatures' flesh to her swallows.

For ten days the ship sailed close-hauled to the trades, flying straight into the wind's eye. The heartwood groaned. Miru worried that the strain would snap the hulls, tear the sails and wrench the masts from their moorings.

One afternoon his sister spied a homing bird high above. "Ru, look!" She leapt and made the birds' calls: "Pi-ru-ru! Pi-ru-ru!"

The next morning Renga Roiti released her two swallows from the cage. When she had almost given up hope for them, when the sun had fallen that day, the birds alighted on the lopped prows, one on each side. The swallows passed the night on the canoe. When they soared away at dawn, Miru steered to follow in their direction.

At death-light the birds returned to the ship again. Miru adjusted the vessel to a starpath in the line of their homing flight, pointing the bow toward the new bearing. The birds might lead the boat to the land where they must be spending mornings and afternoons.

So the journey went for thirteen days. The next morning sharp-eyed Renga Roiti detected a strip of mulberry bark on the water, floating with the current. It reminded her of Mohani and his totems. Her eyes brimmed with tears.

On the fourteenth day beyond the doldrums, at noon, Koro's children spied land. A melancholy smile appeared on Miru's lips when he recognized the naked outline of Motiro—the crag where he had sailed with the crew before they embarked on their mission—the only rock between Vaitéa and the sea-waste.

"Our ship has overshot Vaitéa," he told Renghi. "If it hadn't been for your birds we would have missed our island and the crag too. We would have sailed on forever."

"My swallows have guided us to the nearest piece of land," Renga Roiti acknowledged. Her hollow chest filled with pride.

Brother and sister held each other and said prayers of thanksgiving. They had escaped storms, hunger and death; they were fortunate to have come so far. But they were too ragged and fatigued, too saddened by Mohani's drowning and their other losses to celebrate.

Miru made the canoe come about, running with the southeast trades on a course he knew by heart. For two more nights the swallows homed on their ship. Those birds flew off the next day at dawn.

That evening they did not reappear. "I don't think we'll see my totem sisters tonight," Renga Roiti told her brother. "From now on they'll probably sleep on their new home, Motiro." The young woman missed her swallows deeply.

On the third morning after spotting the barren rock, those seafarers discerned the peak of Terevaka in the fog—the tallest mountain on their island. The sight of their homeland in the sea's embrace brought a flash of joy to their breasts. They hugged.

"*Ma Makemake, ma Tangaroa*," they chanted.

Brother and sister gazed at Vaitéa. After living for months on Ragi, their island looked even more sere, dead and brown than they recalled. Smoke curled upward from one cape to the other. As they drew closer, they saw fires burning before the Living Faces, the stone giants who portrayed their ancestors. More of those statues had been toppled and lay broken on the ground, where piles of corpses surrounded them. Carrying bodies on litters to their graves, men walked back and forth, like ants bearing food to and from their nests.

The captain and Renga Roiti struck sails and dropped masts. With the waves behind them they paddled toward the harbor, where they eased the mutilated bows into the shallows. Their canoe touched land. Miru and his sister sighed, looked at each other and smiled painfully through their cracked, bleeding lips.

Chapter 9

Ariki

Two scrawny boys helped them drag their ship onto the beach. It was a different craft from the sleek boat launched there so many months ago amidst chanting, shaking of shells and pounding of drums, with red and yellow streamers flying in the breeze. Now only a small crowd of people gathered around the battered canoe: hungry children, widows, aged men unfit for war.

Miru cut the cords that secured *Te Roku-o-witi*, and he pulled it free of the housing. Cradling it in both arms, he crawled over the gunnels, followed by his sister, who carried Mohani's rongorongo tablet. When their feet touched ground, the two sailors slumped onto the sand. They leaned against each other as they rose. Groaning with sore muscles, Miru studied the *ao* in his arms. The paddle's sides had been scored, chipped and dented, its polish dimmed by months of being awash in the sea. Tangaroa's wondrous face, etched into the wood, had lost the whaletooth whites and the obsidian pupils of his eyes. Koro's son raised the *ao*, wincing, and let the blade fall into the sand, where it teetered, barely sticking.

He stood on the left side of *Te Roku-o-witi*, his sister on the right. Their legs wobbled. Each extended one arm to the other's shoulder for balance. Those mariners knelt slowly and pressed their foreheads to the soil.

Te Rahai stepped from the crowd. Clotted with dirt, his white hair and beard looked wild. He shuffled to *Te Roku-o-witi* and placed his hand on its weathered wood. He inspected the paddle, the boat, the two sailors.

"Miru and Renga Roiti," he announced in a tremulous voice, "in your father's absence I welcome you home. The gods and the *ao* have granted you a safe return." As Te Rahai embraced his grandchildren, his frame shook. He was too wise to ask about Mohani.

The old man bent down to clench sand in his palms, his bones creaking like the hull of *Mahina-i-te-pua*. Achingly he lifted his body from the ground. As if to scratch the sky, he raised his hands. Te Rahai poured the grains of sand on his head while tears streamed from his eyes. "Your father has been killed," he muttered, "like his two brothers before him."

Renga Roiti sobbed. Miru's knees buckled. No tears warmed his face: he held them back, intent on the purpose of his quest.

"Your mother has changed," Te Rahai went on. "She won't speak to us. She moans and weeps, falls to the floor, starts up and cries 'Koro' and 'Renga Roiti' and 'Miru,' then falls again." The old seaman's stomach growled. Renghi handed him the rongorongo.

Moving arm in arm to keep themselves from falling, Miru and his sister returned to the ship. They climbed below decks to recover Marama's baskets. They took them to the spot where Te Rahai waited by the *ao*. Miru pulled *Te Roku-o-witi* from the sand; he slung it on his shoulder. He and Renga Roiti carried the baskets with their bundles of seeds and shoots. Their weak legs and the knowledge of their father's end seemed to make the earth shift under their feet.

The two shipbuilders had joined the sparse crowd. Both gaped at the longboat. The canoe they had helped fit out for the voyage, the one that used to be so snug and trim, was crippled now, bearded with moss and kelp. They turned their eyes on the pair of young sailors.

"How have they done it?" one of the men asked his companion in a hushed voice. "How could a boy and girl cross the ocean on that boat?"

"Even the great mariners of the past failed," the other said in awe.

Te Rahai told the shipbuilders to find soldiers to protect the canoe against warlords, who would try to break it apart for clubs, spears and shields, for tinder to burn their enemies' houses and their own dead.

As both men kept their eyes trained on Miru and Renga Roiti, one responded, "I would do anything for those two."

Te Rahai doddered in front of his grandchildren, who were also unsteady on their legs. Seen from a distance, they all might have been aged people staggering up the road, holding one another for support. Islanders lowered their heads with reverence and stepped aside for them. The three plodded through parched fields, by empty houses and smoking altars with bodies stacked before them. There were no bushes or trees, only splintered, blackened stumps along the dusty road. Ia's children missed the cool grass under their bare feet on Ragi.

With their heads shaved in bereavement, widows wandered on the roadside, wailing dirges, each clutching her spouse's skull. Clouds of flies fed on the corpses scattered over the earth. A stench of decaying flesh hung in the air.

The seafarers came to the stone well in front of Koro's house. It had crumbled. No dogs slept around it, no pigs rooted, no birds, hens or chicks pecked the dirt. Smoke did not seep through the roofs or the thatch of dwellings on the square.

Sick and pale with grief, Koro's widow sat on the threshold of the great-house with her bald head bowed. Ihu stood at her side. Renga Roiti cried when she saw her mother without her long, shiny braids of black hair. Miru's eyes moistened without dropping tears. He wept inside.

Ia looked up. When she saw her son and daughter, the fountains of her eyes burst. Tall Ihu helped the woman to her feet. She rubbed noses with her children, crying with relief. As if to confirm their presence, she touched their weathered faces, their sun-bleached hair. Mumbling to herself, Ia hugged them tightly.

She tried to recount her husband's death. Her voice no longer sounded like water: it cracked when she spoke. The widow wrung her hands with sorrow. Ihu comforted her.

The priest finished the tale for Miru and his sister. As Koro had foreseen, the Raas had retrieved the sacred egg and won the manbird competition in the spring. The king and his forces seized the opportunity to attack the Tuus, burn their fields, homes and ships. Their father was ambushed and slaughtered by three soldiers, Ihu said, but not before taking some of the enemy down with him. Then the Raas had breached the laws of war by dragging Koro across fields, spitting on his corpse, cursing him and the Tuus. They denied his family its right to receive the victim. Instead they delivered his body to their warlords, men with bloody hands who mocked the slain hero in public, beheaded him, roasted and devoured Koro's flesh. Knowing that a fierce warrior's skull holds mana, they dried and concealed it. Ia did not have the widow's consolation of cradling that noble head in her hands, keening, honoring and burying it herself.

"In spite of your youth," the woman told her son through tears, "you're Ariki now, a lord of our tribe and our family. You must make peace with Koro's memory."

Miru sensed the weight of his father's demise and humiliation. His head still rocked from the voyage.

Ia was too bereft to hear the account of her children's journey. It was enough that they had reached home. With her head hanging she walked to the women's chamber. Renga Roiti followed.

Koro's son turned to the priest. "Ihu, have soldiers take the seeds and shoots to my father's armory and watch over them." For the first time he acknowledged himself as an equal to his uncle.

"Yes, Ariki," the man replied through his grizzled beard. It would take Miru months to grow used to that title that once belonged to Koro.

In the afternoon he left the house with Renga Roiti. He took the rongorongo tablet while she carried *Te Roku-o-witi*. Murmuring under their breath, people on the roads wondered at the children of Ia's milk, who resembled wraiths in a dream.

Like shadows the two approached the no-man's country. Kuihi and Kuaha were waiting for them at a crossroads, seated on two branches of a withered tree, their beards dangling to the earth. Both looked older by years. Instead of waving in the breeze, the tufts of hair in their ears sagged to their shoulders.

"I'm Kuihi," one dwarf said, as if he not met the brother and sister. He leapt from the tree, slipped and tumbled into the dirt.

As though he were addressing strangers, the other echoed, "I'm Kuaha." He jumped, tripped and fell on his twin brother.

"Miru Miru Miru," the first called from the ground, trying to laugh, making a grimace instead.

"Renghi Renghi Renghi," the second added, coughing, the words sticking in his throat.

The twins rose to their feet. As they examined Koro's children, their faces drooped. How bony the brother and sister's bodies! How red their young eyes, scorched by sunlight and mourning! They noticed the air of loneliness surrounding the Ariki.

For their part Miru and Renga Roiti were astonished to see how much the dwarves had changed—they looked hunched and scraggly, with wiry legs like twigs. Kuihi's red hair and goatee had lost their sheen; Kuaha's black hair and beard were flecked with gray. As if the brothers expected to be ambushed, their eyes shifted from one side to the other, their heads twitched, their torsos jerked backward and forward.

One told Miru with a break in his voice, "Come."

"Follow," the other told Renghi with a tear in his eye.

They found the border thick with troops. The dwarves did not disguise brother and sister; Miru and Renga Roiti changed clothes and loosened their braids on their own. Stealthily the four prowled into the heartland.

They passed ruined houses, funeral processions and altars heaped with corpses. When the ground rumbled, and the air reverberated with the crash of collapsing walls, houses and Living Faces, Kuihi and Kuaha cowered, stopping their ears. Those two lizards moved slower, without the old spring in their steps. Despite their sea-worn, blistered bodies, Renga Roiti and Miru kept up with the twins.

The friends passed altars piled with rotting carcasses, buzzing with flies, littered with bones split open and sucked dry of marrow. They heard widows bemoaning their men. Like their own people, brother and sister observed, the Raas had suffered from war and hunger. They remembered Ragi, that island where death did not reek in the air. After surveying the familiar house and the valley, Kuihi and Kuaha smiled weakly at Ia's children, turned and blew away like two clouds in the wind.

Miru and Renga Roiti stood before the threshold, disheartened by the dry well; not a single dog barked or wagged its tail to greet them. No pigs scavenged in the dust. Butterflies no longer fluttered around the door.

They called Neira's name. When she opened, she did not know the two figures, gaunt as ghosts. Finally she recognized Miru and Renga Roiti. In anticipation she looked at them. As soon as she saw their moist eyes, she gushed tears.

"*Aûé!*" Neira screamed, "where is he? *Aûé* Mohani, *aûé!*" She tore at her black hair, streaked with white. She scratched her cheeks. When she struck Miru, he did not resist, letting the woman claw his face, neck and arms until she slumped to his feet. From the ground she scraped his knees and shins feebly, sobbing.

Neira dug into the soil with her fingernails. "*Aûé!* Raunui has lost his only son and Kenetéa her only brother . . . Mohani . . . Moha—"With her mouth pressed to the dust, the woman gagged.

Renga Roiti stroked Neira's hair. "He was our little sea swallow," she told the woman, "our navigator, our singer of starsongs. Without him we could not have reached the island where we found seeds and sprigs to plant on Vaitéa. Mohani died at the helm of our ship. Your son will be remembered."

Miru reached down to touch the woman's head. "Neira," was all he could say. He wished that he could utter winged words like Marama

The boy's mother still cried. Tears, blood and dirt covered her face. She rose haltingly. As if Renghi were a child of her own, Kenetéa's mother embraced her.

Neira released the young woman. His face bleeding where her fingernails had gouged him, Miru handed her the rongorongo. She fondled it with her palms, whimpering, her eyes fixed on the wooden tablet.

Neira glanced up at him. Miru studied her eyes; they were black like Kenetéa's, their whites reddened by tears. She gave him the rongorongo with one hand, wiping blood from his cheeks with the other.

"It's for you and your sister," she said, "who traveled with Mohani. I'm proud he sailed on a mission that could help our island," she ended without conviction.

Miru longed to ask about Kenetéa. He did not, knowing the woman needed to be alone with her pain. He and his sister said goodbye to Neira.

At dusk they reached the secluded grove at Kote Pora, swathed in fog. The forbidden woods, once the densest on Vaitéa, had thinned even more: many trees were withered, others had been chopped down to stumps. After looking closely at Miru and his bloodied visage, the guard ushered Koro's children to the cave. There were no attendants to lead them inside.

Following the sound of crashing surf, Miru and Renga Roiti felt their way through the maze.

As though she expected their arrival, Marama stood waiting at the far end of her grotto, enveloped in sea fog, on a ledge where waves beat against the rocks below. She scrutinized the newcomers with her gray eye, the good one, the color of the mist that swirled around her. Marama's white cloak flapped in the breeze.

"Welcome home, Ariki," she pronounced. "Your face is bleeding like a slaughtered pig's." Miru blushed. "And Renga Roiti," the seer said, "you're a woman now—the first to hold the *ao*." Seeing her red eyes and tear-washed cheeks, Marama added, "Do not worry, my daughter—weeping is a woman's lot."

Hobbling on her staff, Marama approached Renga Roiti, wheezing. Lightly she stroked the young woman's hair, her shoulders and budding breasts. "The *maori* performed his art well," the sorceress said, admiring Renga Roiti's tattoos.

Sister and brother heard the woman's thick breathing. "Children of Ia," Marama said, "gods and goddesses have led you across the sea-waste."

She moved closer and placed one hand on Miru's face. He felt the jagged tips of her fingernails. "Son of Koro, you've begun to fulfill the prophecies. You've surrendered your love for a woman in order to succor our people. Upon your sacrifice the gods themselves throw offerings." The sound of breakers roared through Marama's words.

She paused, still touching his face. "Miru, I wish that I could provide you drink and food worthy of your quest. Wouldn't you love to swallow the sacred kava?" The priestess laughed, remembering his face of chicken dung, his eagerness to drink the beverage in the last rite of manhood. "But there's no more kava and little food or firewood to cook it. The warlords have felled more trees for weapons and for fuel to burn their dead. The people have consumed all the pork, fowl and dogs on the island. Only a few rats remain. And long-pigs, of course." Miru and Renga Roiti looked at each other, baffled by the woman's words.

"You've been away for so many months!" Marama cried. "'Long-pigs' is what the warlords call humans—the last good meat on Vaitéa." Images of Koro's death flitted through the brother's and sister's minds.

"Do you mean that people are eating each other?" Miru asked.

Marama smiled knowingly. She paused to give her silence its full shock to the visitors, who seized one another's hands, trembling.

Marama raised her staff. "Miru, as the prophecies foretold, you've served our people on the sea. It's time for you to serve them on land. You're the chosen one."

Miru made an effort to speak. "I have no more strength," he said slowly. Renga Roiti had never heard him sound so dejected.

"You must draw strength from the earth, my son," Marama said. "It's time for you to plant *Te Roku-o-witi* in the soil." With her white cloak the sorceress made a sweeping whoosh. "It will mark the end of your wanderings and your new tie to the land."

Marama moved closer to Renga Roiti. "Daughter," she started in her sonorous voice, resting one hand on the young woman's shoulder. "You've begun to achieve the prophecy I announced at your birth-feast—that you would help your brother in his sacrifice for Vaitéa."

The seer lowered her staff to the ground. Lifting her free arm, she ordered, "Go now, both of you, and set *Te Roku-o-witi* in the earth. Then plant the shoots and seeds you've brought to our island." The oyster-shells on Marama's ears jangled.

Miru would have liked to recount Mohani's disappearance, the storm, the seeds and sprigs lost at sea. He wanted to tell the priestess that he had failed to find great-palm and coconut. He yearned to describe the spreading tree to her, the spirits who lived around it, who seemed to sing his name. But Miru trusted that his reticence spoke to Marama, that she comprehended without words. He had begun to grasp how wise a woman can become after a hundred years and more.

In fact she had not lost the power to see into his mind. "Someday you'll tell me more," she assured him. When a roller hit the crags, Miru recalled Kenetéa.

The witch divined his thoughts again. "As for the one whose skin is smooth like mother-of-pearl, she must lament for her brother Mohani. Afterward Kenetéa will marry Nuku by the king's order."

Miru gasped like a man struck in the belly. When he faltered at Renga Roiti's side, she gripped her brother's arm.

Always seeking the upper hand, Marama rushed to exploit his weakness: "Kenetéa's betrothed to a mighty man—Nuku's the stoutest warrior, the boldest leader, the strongest swimmer on our island. And there's something else, son of Koro. Another fearless soldier—Raunui—will stalk and slay you as soon as he learns of his son's death." The priestess allowed the force of her words to settle in the young man's mind. "So you must travel to the king's palace in order to retrieve Koro's head before Raunui strikes. Family weighs more than love, friends or enemies, Miru."

He felt as small and unsure as on the first visit to Marama's cavern, when he was a boy who cared only about Kenetéa and his family. Now I'm supposed to save the people and the whole island, he thought, feeling overcome by the seer's words. Then I had hopes of winning the girl's love—I've lost that too. And her father's going to hunt and kill me.

Three times Marama breathed in and out. "It's not easy to become Ariki," she intoned, spreading her white wings. "When you've restored your father's skull, travel one more time to my sanctuary."

With their heads still rocking from the sea, the two sailors reached their house. They had a fitful sleep broken by thunder, lightning, squalls and shrieks of mourning widows. Miru dreamed of Koro's skull and the smell of seaweed on Te Rahai's skin. Renga Roiti also had visions of her father through the night.

They awoke to a drizzly morning. Miru recalled the damp, dreary days after Kenetéa's exile to the virgins' cave. Now he welcomed Hiro's tears, knowing they would help the seeds take root in the soil. As Neira had taught him, Miru placed them in a calabash filled with rainwater, where they could soak and soften before planting.

The family convened in the longroom. Ia, Ihu and Te Rahai stood in a circle around the two young voyagers, who cradled the *ao* in their arms. With Koro gone it seemed many people were missing. Miru could hold back no longer; his tears spilled onto the hearth.

Te Rahai and Ihu faced the brother and sister. Resting a shaky hand on *Te Roku-o-witi*, the old captain said, "Miru, it's time for you to sink the paddle in the hearth." The priest elevated his arms. "Tangaroa," he chanted, watching the ceremonial *ao*, "accept this oar in gratitude for a safe passage over the sea."

Miru lifted the paddle above his head. Heaving a sigh, he drove its blade into the ashes and soil of the hearth, where it teetered. Tall Ihu stepped forward and ground the oar deeper.

While Renga Roiti stayed with the family, her brother walked to the armory at the rear of the house. Two guards removed a large stone that blocked the door. Miru picked up Marama's baskets with their bundles of seeds, saplings and shoots that were stored in the cool darkness. Between trips back and forth to the longroom, a rainy night from long ago returned to his mind, when Koro had given him the knife of obsidian in that place. The weapon had crossed the ocean on the twin-hulled canoe, served him on Ragi and on the inbound journey. In his heart he felt a twinge of pain for his dead father.

With the baskets in their arms Miru and Renga Roiti left the great-houses behind them, the smoking altars, heaps of bodies and howls of distress.

"Renghi," he said, "listen." His brow furrowed.

"What, Ru?"

"The last seeds and shoots of sandalwood died in the storm."

The young woman grabbed her stomach where the tattooer had incised an image of the tree. Her countenance darkened, and she wept.

Miru held out his hands to her. "Come, Renghi." He embraced his sister.

Both turned and stared ahead. In spite of all, the road beckoned. Miru recalled the days when he, Renga Roiti and Kenetéa had explored together, and when he and the thin-ankled girl had found the island of their love. How far away those times seemed to him, the warmth and excitement that filled them.

Still weary from the mission, Ia's children stooped to sow their remaining seeds and set their saplings in the earth. They preferred sheltered places, but they also chose clearings where more sunlight would reach the plants.

Miru dug rows with the knife of obsidian. Renga Roiti laid seeds in the ground. Before planting the shoots she fondled and spoke to them, brushed them against her spindly arms and legs, as though she wanted to leave a part of herself on those sprigs. Softened by autumn rains, the earth opened to receive the new life. At night the children of Ia's milk returned home to rest.

With the dwarves as guides they crossed the no-man's land again. As usual the two lizards vanished when they had performed their task. Miru and Renga Roiti found a spot to sleep by day, hidden from bands of Raa soldiers who were mustering for battle nearby. In the moonlight they planted the last seeds and sprigs.

"Ru," she whispered, "Marama must have ordered the moon to shine for us."

For the first time since they had come back to Vaitéa, he smiled. Both looked up at the sky. A quarter moon shone so clearly that they could discern the outline of its sphere.

"It looks like a mother holding a child in her arms," Renghi said, touching Miru's hand.

The travelers retraced their route home. They saw that the first seeds had already begun to sprout delicate, downy buds. A few saplings had taken root, supple in the soil, bending in the breeze like miniature masts of a canoe. Miru and Renga Roiti rejoiced to see them. But their faces saddened when they noticed a wilted seedling lying on the ground. As they drew close to the border, they saw that more and more young trees had been crushed by the feet of marching warriors.

Chapter 10

Men with Bloody Hands

When Miru and Renga Roiti returned home, they found their grandfather lying on the earthen floor of the longroom. Ihu had moved him to the hearth beside *Te Roku-o-witi*. The shapely oar stood in the soil and ashes where brother and sister had rooted it, where fires used to burn.

They crouched next to Te Rahai. When the old man saw them, his weathered face brightened for a moment. "The ocean can break the strongest heart," he whispered, raising and dropping a shaky hand on his sunken chest. "But the wars and hatred have killed me."

The old seafarer fixed his glazed eyes on Miru. "Turn your back from this evil—do not seek to avenge your father." With a wrinkled hand he pointed to the knife of obsidian sheathed to his grandson's arm. "Break the circle of death, Ariki! Bring peace to our family and our people."

Te Rahai turned to his granddaughter, who leaned over the dying man. "Little bird," he sighed, grazing her forehead with the tips of his shrunken fingers. "My little bird." Renghi fell onto the floor at his side.

Miru helped her to rise. Painfully Te Rahai pulled the boat-shaped amulet over his head. His grandson helped, taking the whalebone piece in his hands, rubbing and looping it around his own neck. He felt the warmth and burden of the *reimiro*, heavier than a stone. He wondered if the sea had burst his own heart—or was it the death of his father, of Kenetéa's love, of Mohani, of so many trees, shoots and seeds?

In the night Te Rahai's soul spun free. His family dressed the corpse in a sash of tree bark. At dawn they carried his body to the harbor. As rain fell like lances, they lowered the old captain into the single-hulled canoe that he had sailed with Miru and Renga Roiti. In it they bore him to the family's burial ground, where the clan's Living Faces stood gazing at the sea. No enemy had shown the courage or strength to topple those statues.

Bearers placed the funeral boat before a stone altar. On either side of it lay piles of carcasses, wrapped in tapa cloth and tied with braids of mourning. White taboo stones marked the precinct.

Hiro's tears poured from the clouds. Miru and Renga Roiti kneeled. Wailing dirges, groups of women, men and children came, their voices muffled by the rain:

> *Aûé, aûé,* what will become of us?
> Alas for us, O captain,
> Father who crossed the sea-roads,
> who brought abundant food,
> many fish, many eels.
> Te Rahai, you are lost to us!
> O father, great fisherman,
> your taut line sang.
> *Aûé, aûé,* what will become of us?

As he listened, Miru thought about his father, who had not been accorded the privilege of a funeral.

Engo appeared at the ceremony with a cadre of troops. While his soldiers stood in the driving rain, the warlord stepped toward Miru. The two young men had not seen one another since the day when *Mahina-i-te-pua* embarked on its voyage. Engo wore a reed helmet topped by a plume of feathers in Tuu yellow. His body bristled with weapons—daggers, a sword, club and spear.

"Ho, Ariki!" the soldier called.

"Ho," Miru responded, wiping tears from his eyes. Through the rain he looked closer at chinless Engo. Battle wounds deformed the tattoos on the warrior's face. Engo's torso looked larger than Miru remembered, rounder than the three sharks incised on his chest and limbs. How could this soldier have grown fatter when the fields were dry and wasted, he asked himself in silence, when the seas were almost fished out, when the people suffered famine?

"Your family has lost two men," the warlord stated, looking at Te Rahai's death-ship. "You're the last male in a long line of ancestors." Engo pointed at the monuments of the Living Faces towering above them, their crowned heads nearly touching the low clouds. "I've come to help you repay your father's murder."

Miru looked at Te Rahai's boat. "Before he died, my grandfather told me not to seek vengeance," he said. Rain fell through his words.

"Miru, those heroes, those Living Faces will think that fright has driven you from just revenge on the Raas. Men who once admired you will treat you with scorn. For a man of honor disgrace is worse than death."

Recalling that Engo had been an orphan for years, Miru tried to suppress his anger. "I've spoken," he told the warrior. When the man began to reply, Miru interposed, "You're profaning my family's burial ground by pressing me to kill." His stomach growled.

The orphan smirked. "If you join us, you'll never know hunger again."

"Go."

Engo turned and departed with his forces.

Miru and other men dragged Te Rahai's death-boat to the harbor. They pushed it through seething surf. Koro's son hurtled himself onto the ship, paddled beyond the waves, looked lovingly for the last time at his grandfather's corpse, jumped overboard and watched the vessel run to sea before he swam to shore.

For days the family mourned. Miru felt alone without an elder in the clan. I'm almost as much an orphan as Engo, he thought. Each night he dreamt of Koro's eyes, gray as winter fogs, and Te Rahai's body, creaking like a ship.

One morning Ia's children dressed their finest. Miru's frame, wizened by sun, storms and grief, no longer filled out his clothes. Renga Roiti had to cut down a cloak of tapa cloth to fit him, dyed in yellow.

Ia attired her daughter in a waistcloth. The garment was alive with memories: it was partly threaded from the dark-brown hair she had sheared from her own skull at her husband's death. Over it Renghi wore a cloak stained with turmeric, tied to her shoulder with a whaletooth pin fashioned in the shape of a sooty tern. Ia and Koro had saved this talisman for their daughter's passage to womanhood.

When brother and sister stepped from the great-house, his *reimiro* and her totem pin flashed in the sunlight. They crossed fields where they had set their shoots and seeds. A few more had sprouted, but most had failed to strike roots, shriveling in the soil from lack of rain. Others had been trampled. As far as they could tell, all the tender toromiro had perished. Only a few hibiscus, mulberry and offshoots of the spreading tree remained.

Renga Roiti kneeled next to the live seedlings, urging them to grow, cooing and billing as she did for her birds. Miru also spoke to the saplings as though they were his sons or daughters. Recalling Raunui and Koro, he knew the pain a father could feel for his children. His sister watched him closely. Grooves creased Miru's brow, reminding her of the furrows where the young plants grew or lay dying.

They reached the royal sanctuary at Anakena. The palace was surrounded by a wall of white taboo stones. With their spears raised, a line of soldiers halted the visitors.

Miru faced them. "I'm Ariki."

"I've never seen such a skinny lord," the leader responded, snickering. "And he has freckles too!" His warriors laughed. The man spit on the earth before admitting Miru and Renga Roiti to the grounds. As she passed with the bright-yellow cloak draped from her shoulder, the leader and his troops ogled her. Miru stared at them in turn.

More soldiers met the strangers before the stone longhouse. It was built by the founders in the shape of an upturned canoe, thatched with a tightly woven roof of reeds and stalks of sugarcane. It overlooked the cove and the beach of pink sands where the first king had made landfall on Vaitéa. Miru remembered the invaders on the green island.

Escorted by a pair of guards, he and Renga Roiti approached the threshold of the palace. Its door jambs were sculpted with high-prowed ships, manbirds and sacred eggs, turtles and rooster heads. Leading sister and brother inside, both warriors snarled at them. Miru almost said something; instead he merely glared, biting his tongue.

The royal chamber swarmed with people. On one side women agitated strings of seashells while men danced on percussion plates of calabash. On the other priests and nobles, seated on mats of soft pandanus, intoned chants and swayed to the cadence of drums. Male and female servants crossed in all directions.

King Hiti sat in the rear on an elevated throne, eating from a plate piled with clams, sea urchins and lobsters. Facing him, brother and sister saw long tables loaded with clusters of bananas and fresh shoots of sugarcane, baskets and trays of eels, oysters, mussels, yams, taro and sweet potatoes. They had not seen such food anywhere, not even on Ragi.

A chamberlain entered the large room. He was an old man who wore a turtle pendant around his neck. "Is this your first audience with King Hiti?" he asked the newcomers.

"Yes," the two answered as one.

"You must stand clear of the throne. Do not touch the chief's body or anything that has come into contact with the regal person. He is inviolate." As the chamberlain spoke, Miru and Renga Roiti watched servers heaping trays of food on a pedestal before the king.

The elderly man guided those sailors to a row of taboo stones around the throne. After announcing their arrival the chamberlain shuffled to one side and squatted on a reed mat. Ia's children paced toward the ruler.

Hiti dusted scraps of food from his belly. With blank eyes he seemed to look down at the pair of Tuus. "May your grandfather's soul spin free," a small voice piped from his plump torso. "Te Rahai was a wise seaman. When I was a young prince I allowed him to fish for tuna in the royal reserves off Anakena." The chief shifted his body in the throne carved with shapes of sea turtles; as though it would collapse under his weight, its frame squeaked. Hanging on his neck, six wooden balls, each with tassels of pandanus, clinked and jostled.

"Hiti," Miru began, using a noble's privilege of addressing the king without a title. "We've come to speak with you about another man—our father." Renga Roiti nodded. "Koro was slain by Raa soldiers who flouted the laws of warfare. They beheaded him, roasted and ate his body. They haven't taken his head to our mother."

"Greed for long-pig has also been a sin of Tuu warriors," Hiti declared. "Blood will have blood." He turned his empty eyes away. "The manbird has become nearly as dominant as the king." Nuku's father sounded as if he were talking about the chief of another island, not Vaitéa. "How can a king rule if people worship the sacred egg as much as their monarch, as Makemake and Tangaroa?" he asked the brother and sister. "The manbird controls many of the warlords and their blood-oath. The chief cannot rein in the soldiers of his own tribe, much less yours. The gods are different now—none of my priests can explain it." His voice fell off, stifled in the clamor of shells and drums.

Hiti looked toward the visitors as though his dead eyes could see them. "My emissaries have told me that you sailed to an island." He pronounced these words vaguely, without interest or expecting a response. The chamberlain had fallen asleep on the reed mat.

Keen-witted Renghi touched Miru's arm. Their eyes met; after months together on the quest they could speak to one another without words. Their looks said that it would be useless to tell the blind king about their journey, the seeds, sprigs and shoots that might restore the woods on Vaitéa.

"Why are you here?" Hiti inquired. He spoke as if he had just wakened from a dream.

"We've come to retrieve Koro's skull!" Renga Roiti cried, rubbing the waistcloth woven from her mother's hair.

Hiti raised a large wooden staff from his side and swatted his chamberlain. The old man startled. "Take them to the prince," the chief ordered.

"Which, my lord?"

"Nuku, of course." The king yawned.

Without saying farewell, Miru and Renga Roiti followed the old man. They passed through a wide door, stepped onto a terrace and saw the view of Anakena, its green cove and pink sands. Talking in groups, guards loitered on the palace grounds. The chamberlain told the travelers to wait. He doddered back to the stone longhouse.

In the sunlight Miru and his sister regarded each other. Their eyes asked, How could that obese, sightless man be the descendant of our hero kings? What happened to our chiefs with their old wisdom and greatness?

"Hiti's blind in more than one way," Renga Roiti whispered. "He doesn't see what's occurring on our island."

"At least he knows the gods are changing, that people worship the manbird more than the king now."

"My brother—" she spurted, nearly choking. "How can they gorge themselves in the palace while our people go hungry?"

Miru recalled Engo, stout as a great-shark. "The warlords also eat well. Someday that will change," he said, peering beyond the bay.

The ground shook. Moving like a forest of spears, a phalanx of troops advanced toward the terrace. The palace guards scattered. Those marching soldiers circled Koro's children, forming a ring from whose center emerged Nuku. On his head he wore a reed helmet, crowned with tall plumes, dyed in Raa red. A necklace of obsidian, polished to a brilliant black, fell over his chest, where a tattooed volcano spouted lava. The prince's loins were girded by heavy folds of bark-cloth and braided tassels. Rings of human hair encircled his ankles and thighs. His left hand hung free, while the other held a lance, hewn from sandalwood, the top sharply pointed, the bottom rounded like a paddle blade.

"Ho, Ariki!" he called Miru. The king's son knew the courtesies.

Miru greeted the man who would marry Kenetéa. "Ho."

The prince nodded to Renga Roiti, who looked small and out of place in that circle of armed men. The plumes of their helmets, dyed red like Nuku's, fluttered in the breeze. Streaked by trickles of sweat and blood, their bodies were coated in layers of dust. Those warriors must have arrived straight from the battlefield.

"Nuku," Koro's son said, "my father was slain by your soldiers, who defiled his corpse, cooked and ate it."

"They haven't restored his head to our mother," Renga Roiti added, fondling her dark cloak. She was not a bit cowed by the king's son or his troops.

With eyes the color of oyster shells, Nuku looked down at the newcomers; unlike his father's, his were alive. He inhaled deeply. "A great warrior's head holds mana. I'll have Koro's skull returned." Miru detected a smile on the prince's face. As real as if she were there in person, he sensed the white-armed girl between them. The sun beat on their heads.

Nuku coughed before replying. "Many things have changed since you departed on your voyage, Ariki. Soldiers on both sides have killed, dishonored, tortured and enslaved their enemies. We've burned each other's crops and eaten long-pig. Blood of the two tribes has soaked the earth." Nuku rubbed his black necklace with fingers rounder than stalks of sugarcane.

When Miru pictured those hands on Kenetéa's skin, pale as the moon, his stomach turned. He waited before speaking. "As our grandfather was dying," Miru said, "he told us not to seek vengeance for my father's death." He felt the pull of the old man's *reimiro* around his neck.

"May his soul spin free," Nuku said.

"'Break the circle of death!' That's what Te Rahai told us."

"'And bring peace to our family and our people,'" Renghi put in, refusing to be shunned in that council of males. Waves lapped on the beach.

Nuku pawed the ground with one foot, swishing the braided tassels on his leg, thick as a tree trunk. "Ariki, it's too late for one or two men to bring peace. There are forces larger than us and our tribes."

"I know. Look at the cove of Anakena behind you." Miru swept his hand in an arc. Some warriors stepped aside to leave a view of the pink-sanded beach, its green shallows and the deep blue water beyond.

Nuku did not bother to look at the sea. "I was born here," he said. "I've seen it almost every day of my life." A few soldiers chuckled.

Miru stared straight at the king's son. "You and the Raas, the Tuus also, we've looked at the ocean without seeing it. It and the earth are the forces greater than our tribes. If we don't care for them, we'll die. All of us." Seeing the warlord's gray, unmoving eyes, Miru wished that he could speak with the music of words like Marama.

"Ariki," the prince began, "I've heard about your quest. Nobody but you could have made such a crossing—you're the last man of boats."

Renga Roiti cried: "I also sailed on the voyage!"

Some of the warriors sniggered. Nuku muzzled them with a turn of his shoulder and a withering look. He faced the visitors again, his eyes landing on Renga Roiti. "What did you find on that island?"

Before she could respond, Miru intervened: "Only a few seeds and shoots."

"On the day of your launching," Nuku said, "you agreed to offer whatever you found for partition between the tribes."

"We never agreed to that," Miru responded. "Your brother Kaimokoi proclaimed it. Besides, there's nothing to offer. We were fortunate to return from Ragi with our lives and a battered ship. Mohani was not so lucky." Miru looked for a reaction in the face of the warlord who would soon marry the drowned boy's sister; the man showed none. Had Nuku even learned about Mohani's death?

The king's son waited before speaking. Through the slits of his eyes he glared down at Miru. "You could return to Ragi with more women, men and children from your tribe."

Gazing at Nuku, Koro's son replied without words: *How I hate to hear that island's name on your tongue.*

The prince was too confident to feel menaced by Miru's silence or his look. "Such a mission could bring peace," he said with composure. "You could be a hero king like our founder, like our ancestors."

Miru smiled sadly. "I'm not a hero or a king, Nuku. My sister and I have planted the *ao* in the hearth of our longhouse. By doing it we pledged to stay and help our island."

As a gull dove and screeched above him, the warlord considered. "Miru, when we were children you saved my brother in high surf one day. Now you've made a journey across the seas—the bluewater and the trade winds belong to you. Flee to Ragi!" The prince's hoarse shout grated on Miru's ears.

"We shall not leave Vaitéa," the Ariki answered. Only he and his sister knew how impossible, calamitous, how unthinkable a second voyage would be.

Renga Roiti stepped forward, appearing tiny in that press of soldiers. "Nuku," she said, "you've just recalled the time my brother rescued Kaimokoi in the waves. We're asking you to follow the same feeling that led Miru to save a man of another tribe—a spirit of peace."

As usual the king's son delayed before speaking. In order to prepare his audience, Nuku surveyed them, set his teeth and expanded his chest; one of his weaknesses was a fondness for solemnity. "Ariki and Renga Roiti," he started, "our island can no longer feed two tribes. My people own the dark earth and we shall hold it. You have the wide ocean—sail on it or die."

"We stay," Renga Roiti affirmed.

King Hiti's son ignored the young woman, looking at Miru for a response.

"We've spoken," the Ariki said.

A cricket sang in the dry grass. Releasing a sigh, Nuku said, "You've declined the only peace I can propose. If you and your people don't leave Vaitéa, we must face each other in combat. Our tribe has already dashed yours on the battleground. We've scorched your fields and crops." Big-armed Nuku paused. Koro's son clenched his teeth and fists. "You must know that we've won the manbird competition again and the winner has acquired more power. Some of your warlords have sworn allegiance to him." When the prince stopped for a second time, sounds of shells and drumbeats floated from the royal house. "In the spring I'll enter the contest myself," he went on, "to ensure that there will be a Raa manbird for another year. By then the island will be mine . . . and my people's." A murmur rose from the thronged warriors.

Miru's nostrils quivered. "Nuku! You're as blind as your father." The prince was not used to hearing insults; his jaw tightened, his muscles tensed, and he rose on the balls of his feet. "You and I belong to the same people," Miru told him. "And we all belong to this earth," he added, stomping the ground. "And to that sea." Miru pointed to the bay.

"Farewell," the king's son called as though he had heard nothing. At a twist of Nuku's head the soldiers sprang to attention, raised their spears, let out a deep-voiced cry in unison and marched off in double file. The ground trembled, and dust clouded the air. Beyond the white taboo mounds those warriors disappeared.

Miru and his sister stood alone on the terrace above the beach at Anakena. They looked at each other.

"You were brave, Renghi."

She lifted her head with pride. "Ru, those men don't understand."

"No. They're not friends to the world."

"They're men with bloody hands—no better or worse than Engo and the Tuu warlords." A seagull circled above, banked, squealed and flew away. "Nuku's like that bird," Renga Roiti said.

"Why?"

"Because he looks beautiful but when he opens his mouth, he squawks like a gull." Both smiled.

Escorted by a squad of warriors bearing spears, Kaimokoi arrived at their great-house in the morning. He carried Koro's skull enveloped in the finest tapa cloth.

The younger prince unwrapped the soldier's head. It was burnt, cracked, incised and painted red with Raa clan-signs in Koro's blood. The king's son proffered it to Ia, who stood between her children and Ihu at the threshold.

The widow shrieked. Kaimokoi and his warriors started, plugging their ears against the woman's cries. Ia rushed into her house.

The prince faced Miru. "Ariki, I'm ashamed of what my people have done." He tendered the skull.

Feeling the weight of his father's head in his hands, Miru was too shaken to respond. First he tried to suppress his tears. "Kaimokoi," he uttered, "my grandfather urged me not to seek revenge." He coughed to keep from crying. "But if your tribe breaches the laws of war, dishonors my father and my family—how long can I refrain?" Miru's voice carried across the dusty square.

"Ariki, there's something I want to tell you and your sister." Kaimokoi looked at his soldiers and Ihu, the remaining bystanders. The tall priest understood; he entered the house while the warriors withdrew beyond hearing. The king's son remained alone with Miru and Renga Roiti on the threshold.

Kaimokoi took a deep breath. "Nuku's scouts have spotted you on our tribal lands." Waiting for a response, he hesitated. There was none. "My brother has sent soldiers to uproot and burn whatever you planted in our soil."

In her anger Renga Roiti's face turned redder than her hair. Still holding his father's skull, Miru regarded Kaimokoi with a look that must have pierced the man. He felt his old fury against Nuku and the Raas. But he reflected before speaking. "My sister and I brought seeds and shoots from a green island to renew our forests. Most were lost at sea. We've planted the rest in Tuu and Raa soil—some have already shriveled from the drought." Miru paused. "Others have been crushed by marching soldiers."

He placed one hand on the prince's arm. "Kaimokoi, all the sprigs and shoots of your totem, the toromiro, have died." Like a wounded man the king's son flinched and clutched his shoulders, marked by tattoos of that sturdy tree. The manbird wished to console him. "At least some native toromirus have survived on our island," he offered.

Miru allowed time for the prince to recover. "Kaimokoi, you tell us that Raas are pulling and scorching the few sprouts that are left. We don't have the forces to safeguard those young trees on your lands. If they die, your forests will vanish." He paused once more. "Can you stop Nuku from killing the shoots and saplings?"

Kaimokoi considered. "He commands most of our army. If he knew I opposed him, he'd have his troops burn the fields from spite."

Miru's eyes were still trained on the prince. "Kaimokoi, I want you to patrol the stands of seedlings on Raa lands." He pronounced those words in a steady tone that Renghi had not heard in her brother's voice. A tingle of fear ran over her skin.

The breeze ruffled Kaimokoi's hair. "Ariki," he said, "you know Nuku's strength. You also know that my word's as true as the toromiro tree." He touched the twigs and leaves of the totem etched on his shoulders. "I'll do whatever's in my power to help."

"Can there be a truce between our tribes?" Miru asked, stroking the crown of his father's skull.

"I know my brother and our warlords, Ariki. No—there can't be a truce," Kaimokoi answered with resignation. The two young men stood motionless, looking into each other's eyes. The king's son turned slowly and left the house.

"Can we trust him?" Renga Roiti asked her brother.

"Did you see his eyes?"

"Yes." Renga Roiti blushed. "They're brown like toromiro bark—with a glitter inside."

"That's not what I meant, sister. His gaze was firm and he looked straight into my eyes." Through his sadness Miru attempted to smile. "Renghi, it's dangerous to have tender feelings for a Raa."

"You remember that too."

"Thank you, sister." Turning serious again, Miru said, "Without Kaimokoi's help we can't protect the seedlings."

He acted swiftly. After placing his father's skull at the hearth, he called Ihu, ordered the priest to post sentries and declare that all saplings were protected. He dispatched his sister and the two old mariners to Kote Pora, where they entreated Marama to do the same.

That night Miru had dreams of Koro's charred, fractured skull. He also dreamt of sap rising through the seedlings' trunks and limbs.

The next day Renga Roiti and the sailors returned from the seer's grotto. She reported that Marama had agreed to help. But the priestess had only a single soldier to keep vigil on her grounds, the same man who guarded the entrance to her cave.

"It's not enough," Miru said.

"I told her that." Renghi wavered for a moment. "She whispered a secret in my ear."

"What?"

"She said for you to remember the spirits." Peering into Renga Roiti's eyes, green like the cove of Anakena, he pondered if she could know about the graceful beings on Ragi.

Brother and sister ranged the no-man's land, where they breathed in the bitter scent of burning leaves. The earth smoldered under their feet. To Renga Roiti and Miru it seemed those fires were consuming their own lives and their people's along with the tender trees. Silently they wept.

Led by the twins again, they reached Kenetéa's house. The dwarves disappeared in the valley. When they met Neira by the well, Ia's children comforted the woman a second time for her loss.

After she had grown calm, Miru announced, "Nuku is torching the new trees." Although he attempted to conceal his outrage, his face revealed it.

Neira sighed for the trees that she loved deeply. "The king's son will be Kenetéa's husband soon," she said, "but the earth is foremost. I know women who'll help me to safeguard the trees."

Sister and brother looked at each other, perplexed. They did not comprehend how Neira and those women could prevent armed warriors from destroying the fragile seedlings.

Sensing their doubts, Raunui's wife said, "Most of those friends are mothers who have lost sons and mates to war. They know our forests—they're healers like me."

Neira eyed Miru. "I must talk to you," she told him. Turning, she glanced toward Renga Roiti, who hung her lip and walked away from the house.

"Go to Ana o Keke," the woman murmured in Miru's ear, squeezing his arm. "Be careful, my son. The white virgins' cave is still guarded closely."

After taking his leave of Neira, Miru joined his sister, who pretended she was not devoured by curiosity.

When they reached their house, Renghi looked into her brother's eyes. "Is there anything you want to tell me, Ru?"

"No."

He set out before daybreak. He walked through dry fields and barren woods. In spite of his sea-worn, blistered body, Miru managed to move with speed, driven by his desire to see Kenetéa. He no longer needed the dwarves to disguise and lead him across the border. By late afternoon he had reached a trail shrouded in fog.

Skirting cliffs that reared above the sea, the path was narrow, hardly wide enough for one man. Offshore winds and updrafts whipped Miru. He stumbled, fell and strove to keep his balance. Through the mist the sun looked white and dim as a moon. By the time he saw the first trees of the taboo grove, the day had almost gone.

Miru slunk through the death-light. He stepped softly so that he would not rustle leaves on the forest floor. Fog billowed around him while the wind howled, and rollers smashed against the rocks below.

It was night when Miru came to a clearing surrounded by walls of crumbled stone. Through an opening he sighted a pair of sentries on their rounds. They called their watch in voices deadened by the mist.

He heard light footfalls. The darkness seemed to shimmer, and Miru's heart fluttered. He could not see her—the moon had not risen, starlight scarcely pierced the clouds and trees—yet he knew that she was near. He moved forward, and their bodies met.

Embracing, they rubbed noses. Miru felt her skin against his own, quivering, smooth as mother-of-pearl. His hands moved down Kenetéa's sides, grazing the bones of her ribcage, her slim waist, her hips. He inhaled the scent of her hair that fell in waves on her shoulders, the fragrance of her limbs sleeked with oil. His head swooned.

Finally he said it: "Téa." He waited. When she did not reply, Miru asked, "Are you truly here or am I dreaming you?"

"I'm here. It's a dream too." Her voice seemed different, neither a girl's nor a woman's, dark and muted, as though it had crossed miles of dense fog.

"This meeting has happened over and over in my mind," Miru said. They held onto each other, and Kenetéa's tears burned his cheeks. "Mohani was our singer and navigator," he said with a pull on his heart, guessing now why Neira had sent him to see her daughter. He gulped to keep his voice from breaking. "Without your brother's starsongs we couldn't have found Ragi, the green island."

Sobs shook Kenetéa. "My little Mohani."

"'My sea swallow,' Renga Roiti used to say. I called him my mulberry shoot."

"Tell me how he died."

"A storm wave swept him away while he was at the helm of our ship. He drowned like a sailor."

For a moment there was silence around them, without the sound of wind or breakers beating the coastline. Kenetéa felt like a small girl who was lost in the immense night of the world. Swallowing her pain, she said, "Mohani's gone and so is your father."

"My grandfather too." Miru touched the whaletooth talisman around his neck.

"And my father will never be solaced for losing his only son. If you only knew how much he loved Mohani, how much he missed him during the voyage, how he longed to be with him again."

Kenetéa and Miru cried for the deaths in their families. She nestled closer. They held each other tightly. If there had been moonlight, they would have cast one shadow.

She sensed Miru's solitude. He knew her sorrow. Kenetéa took one of his hands in hers and placed it on her breast, covered by her sweeping hair. He would have liked for her to hold it there always.

Without speaking, they stood together. Wind moaned in the woods. Kenetéa dropped Miru's hand from her chest.

He cleared his throat. "Téa, when will you leave the white virgins' cave? I've lost count of the months."

"When they heard about Mohani's death, my mother and father asked me to stay here longer. It's the safest spot on our island."

"Things are falling apart. Your tribe is ruled by men with bloody hands. They'll never make peace."

"Your tribe also has men whose hands are stained red." Miru did not reply. Kenetéa touched the *reimiro* around his neck. "You're Ariki now."

"It's like a stone on my shoulders."

"The prophecies foretold that you would make a sacrifice for our people. You've made it at a great price, I know."

"Renga Roiti and I have planted seeds and sprigs to restore the woodlands." Miru paused. "Téa, there were no great-palms on the green island." Smothering a cry, she lowered her head and wept. Kenetéa stroked the tattoos of branches, tendrils, leaves and twigs on her skin. "But we dug seedlings of your other spirit tree," Miru added to comfort her. She caressed the images of hibiscus on her limbs. "We stored them on our ship and rooted them in the soil. Some have wilted and died, thirsty for rain. Others have been burned or trampled by Raa soldiers."

Kenetéa heaved a sigh. Looking up, she asked, "Did you find Mohani's totem trees on the island?"

"We found mulberries—a few survived the journey and they're planted in the ground—but not a single coconut. We also brought back some offshoots of a great tree that had never grown on Vaitéa. They, the mulberry and hibiscus are all that's left."

Miru knew that he should not hurt Téa more. But his anger made him speak: "Nuku's soldiers are the ones who've squashed and torched the seedlings." She looked down again. "Do you plan to marry him?"

The petals of her lips trembled. Breakers crashed below.

Miru's anger swelled: "Téa! Will you marry the man with bloody hands?"

Her tongue darted from her mouth. "My father and King Hiti have ordered me to wed the prince." Miru could barely hear her thin voice. "I cannot disobey them."

In the pit of his stomach he felt sick. Kenetéa seemed far from him, remote in the faint starlight. Stepping back, as though he were seeing her for the last time, he gazed at the young woman. A wave of her black hair covered a corner of one eye. Her pointed breasts rose and fell with her breathing. The curved vines and branches of her tattoos swayed below her belt, down her thighs to her ankles and toes.

A sentry called out in the woods. Another responded.

"I'm afraid for you," she said softly, clutching Miru and listening for footsteps. "Can I ask you something, Ru?" When he heard his secret name on Kenetéa's lips, the hair on his arms stood up.

"What?"

"Would you travel to the sacred mountain?" She looked straight into Miru's wide-open eyes. "Walk to the volcano at Rano Raraku and climb to the crater's top. Pray to both of our gods there. Then you'll know what to do." He could feel her warm breath on his face. "You'll find a way—not Marama's or mine or your family's. Yours."

The sentries approached, their feet crunching dead leaves. Miru and Kenetéa pulled gently apart. Moist from perspiration and tears, their flesh stuck for a moment.

All he could say was her name. "Téa."

"Ru. Remember the woods and fields and shore." She turned and walked away.

Miru watched her vanish in the forbidden grove. He started to follow but heard footsteps behind him; he spun, crouched and saw troops emerging from the thicket. When they had gone, Miru retraced his path along the precipice. Fog swirled, winds buffeted him, and moisture beaded on his first growth of beard.

He tottered around a bend. His hands holding onto the sheer rock for balance, he thought of leaping down the cliff face. But Miru recalled Kenetéa's last words. He also pictured Renga Roiti and his mother at the hearth of their great-house; shadows of his father, Te Rahai and Mohani flitted through his mind too. He set out for home.

Chapter 11

Knives of Obsidian

Famine was on the loose, prowling over Vaitéa, stalking the people. Children expired with their small fists clenched, trying to hold the last warmth of life. At their hearths shrunken men curled up like little boys and surrendered their last breath. Women slipped away to die in the confinement rooms where they had once given birth. Orphans wailed, widows howled, new afflictions struck the islanders.

After setting fire to the new trees in their own territory, Raas began burning those on Tuu lands. The people and a few appointed watchmen were almost helpless to stop them. Miru and Renga Roiti walked through fields that were shrouded with ashes.

Breathing in the scent of scorched sap, leaves and wood, they did not weep as they walked together. They had cried for the mutilation of their ship on the green island, for Mohani's drowning, the lost seeds and shoots, their father's murder and disgrace, their mother's bereavement, their tribe's defeats and hunger, the death of Te Rahai. Miru had also shed tears for Kenetéa, and Renghi for her own reasons. Like the wells and springs of their island, like Hiro's clouds, the fountains of their eyes were empty now, dry as the cracked soil. Or perhaps their tears flowed inward, scalding their young hearts. In sixteen years Miru had known a life's worth of misfortune. And Renga Roiti in eleven summers!

They reached Kote Pora. Saplings fumed around them. A guard accompanied sister and brother to the cave.

Again Marama surprised them from behind. "Ariki!" her voice boomed in the chamber, drowning the sea roar. She ignited a torch in her hand. "You have one more task—the most urgent of all." The witch stalled so that Miru would have to wait to hear what followed. "You must join forces with Engo and conquer the Raas in a decisive battle."

"All the warlords have bloody hands," Miru reacted. "I won't fight with those men or against them."

"You have no choice—either you resist or die. Aren't you Koro's son?"

"I'm also Ia's son," he answered, touching Renghi's hand in the darkness.

"Your mother wanted you to be a sailor, like her father Te Rahai," the priestess said, still ignoring Miru's sister. "You've accomplished her dream. Your father wanted his son to be a soldier, like himself. Now you can follow his desire." The seer paused. "At your birth I predicted you would aid our people first by sea, later by land. The time has come for you to fulfill the prophecies."

"The warlords can't see beyond the battlefield. Can you, Marama?"

With her free hand the seer pointed to the lid of her good eye, the left. "With this I can see far into the future, Miru."

"Everything is changing."

"What are you trying to tell me?" Waves hissed through Marama's utterance.

Miru smiled. He withheld his reply to keep the old hag in suspense. Renga Roiti grazed her brother's hand, proud that he was holding his own against the sorceress.

"Don't try to pull my own tricks on me," Marama told him, waving her torch. "Spit out your words!"

"Can't you steal my thoughts?" Miru inquired.

"There's nothing to steal."

"Then why are you so eager for me to speak?"

Marama was quivering with rage. Renghi leaned forward in expectation.

"Talk, boy," the witch commanded, "or leave my sanctuary!" Marama pointed her sputtering torch at the cave's exit.

Before the quest that order would have wounded him. Now it did not hurt, and Miru smiled again. "All I know is that I must find another way—not yours or my father's."

"Whose?"

Miru recalled Kenetéa's entreaty in the taboo grove. "Mine," he answered. He thought that he could still feel the young woman's breast where she had placed his hand. Was she merely a specter, he asked himself, a creature who disappeared in daytime as suddenly as she had appeared at night?

"Stop dreaming about the white-armed girl!" Marama shouted. She grinned: "Just in case you believe I've lost my power to snatch your thoughts."

"So you admit that I have thoughts now?"

For a second Marama could not find words. "A boy of sixteen is not old enough to think deeply or to find his own way."

"I managed to find my way across the seas—with my sister's and Mohani's help."

"Only because I charged the goddesses and gods to lead you."

Miru considered before replying. "I know the gods who led us on our voyage—Tangaroa and Makemake. Who are the goddesses?"

"What if I don't feel like telling you?" But Marama could not resist displaying her knowledge for long: "They're the spirits who fled Vaitéa," she said, "when our people spoiled their shores and woods—the sacred spots where they used to live."

"I saw those goddesses on Ragi," he said.

"I also sighted them!" Renga Roiti exclaimed, reaching for her brother's arm.

"They won't come back to Vaitéa," the priestess declared without acknowledging the young woman's words. Addressing only Miru, she added, "Unless you conquer the Raas, that is, making the prophecies true."

"No."

The sorceress smiled. "Then the spirits will not return to their shelters on our island home. Your brain's in the clouds, Miru. Come down to earth while there's still time."

"Marama!" he cried. "You and Kenetéa are the ones who taught me about the earth—the sky and ocean too. Have you forgotten the three baskets of your teaching? The rope of wisdom?"

Moon-faced Marama laughed; the sound echoed through the chamber. "At least one of my prophecies will come true—that you'll always be stubborn, Miru! The last time you rejected me, when you were still a boy, you returned to hear my call. Events will prove me right once more. You'll come crawling back to my cave." The seer paused. "Son of Koro, the Raas are winning the war and destroying the seeds and shoots you planted. If the Tuus vanquish our enemies in battle, the youthful trees may survive to reforest our woods and save our island."

Ia's children stood without responding. Water dripped from the cavern walls.

Miru spoke finally. "Can't you see, Marama? War has destroyed the groves and beaches where those goddesses lived." Renghi brushed his hand again. "The spirits won't return unless we stop both armies—Raas and Tuus, all the soldiers who defile those places and stain them with blood."

Marama fumed silently, mouthing the air as if she could not articulate a response.

He stepped closer. Miru breathed in her scent of smoke and ashes. "In your sanctuary," he said, "I passed the rite of manhood. You taught me that we must heal the earth and sea. I'm grateful for all you've done for me and our people, Marama. Now I'm old enough to follow my own mind."

"Ariki," the seer said, aware that she was losing him, finding words at last: "your mother begged you to make peace with your father's memory. There's only one way for you to do that—fight the Raas. The final moment has arrived for our island." Marama's voice faded. Brother and sister had never heard the sorceress speak in that tone, feeble and desperate.

"A peace made through war will not last," Miru stated firmly.

"Old one—" Renga Roiti broke in, "haven't you seen that only brambles grow where soldiers have camped? Haven't you noticed that bad harvests follow in an army's wake?"

"I did not ask you, girl," the priestess muttered, sounding defeated.

"We've spoken," Miru said. "My sister and I have nothing more to say."

"Go then, Ariki," Marama moaned with the melancholy of a hundred years and more. She extinguished the torch in her hand.

Miru wheeled and strode away in the darkness. Renga Roiti followed him down the tunnels, through the cave mouth, into the burning woods and the hazy light of afternoon.

"Ru," she started, squinting her eyes in the smoke. "Marama can't bear for you to go against her will."

"The woman needs to hold onto something. She's alone on an island that's crumbling around her."

"She didn't talk with her winged words tonight."

"No. She's almost as blind as Hiti and the warlords."

Renga Roiti stopped between a pair of trees, where ashes floated in a beam of light from the falling sun. "Why didn't you tell me that you saw the spirits on Ragi?"

153

Miru halted too. "Sometimes I thought they were a dream." From the forest they heard groans of dying soldiers. "No wonder those goddesses have deserted Vaitéa," he said, listening closely. The sounds of torment waned. "Renghi, where did you see the spirits on the green island?"

"Near the roosts of my land-birds, the owls and parrots. Those goddesses glided in and out of trees. I also glimpsed them by the shore— by the mating ground of my sooty terns. I could only see the spirits when I looked sideways."

"I know."

The next day Miru awoke early. He drank water but did not eat. He lashed his knife to one arm, slung a cape over his shoulder, left the house and took a trail to the mountain. Passing toppled statues and bodies that smoldered on the ground, he did not move his eyes from the road.

Only once did Miru look away—when he heard a mother singing a lullaby. She sat on the threshold of a ravaged hut, where dried bones, shreds of clothing and broken weapons littered the ground. In her arms she held a small wooden cradle as she sang.

> Sleep, little one,
> cry no more.
> I will search for sweet grass
> and sugarcane.
> Do not cry, little one.
> Men with bloody hands
> will hear us.
> Rest now, my child,
> weep no more.

Miru could not tell if the infant was alive or dead. In his heart he felt grief and shame for his people.

He arrived at the foot of Rano Raraku. He scaled the volcano's flank, home of the Living Faces. Those giants of stone guarded the way; some stood erect on wooden rails, others leaned on rubble or were prone with their broad backs to the sky. Around them lay tools overgrown with weeds—picks, hammers, chisels. Higher on the slope Miru saw statues facing up, their features almost completed, waiting for their stone keels to be cut free of the quarry. Others had just been started when they were abandoned, hardly separated from the bedrock. They belonged more to the mountain than to men.

He closed his eyes. Miru recalled a time when the volcano hummed with noise, resonating with the sound of hammer blows, echoing with the voices of stonecutters who carved the Living Faces, priests who dedicated those monuments, teams of carriers who hauled them to sanctuaries throughout Vaitéa. How could he have known those days were gone forever?

He climbed to the volcano's rim. When Miru looked out at the horizon, it seemed that he could see to the end of the world. He surveyed the island, its coast and the crater-lake below, that eye of water. He studied it all—Marama's three baskets, one each for the earth, ocean and sky. He saw his homeland, circled with bright surf, the deep blue beyond. He spotted clouds of dust where soldiers fought, fires and smoke where precious seedlings burned.

He chose a place that was neither too high nor too low. Miru set his cape there. He squatted and let the sun warm his body. In the weeds a cricket chirped. He picked up a stone, a fire-rock that once had spewed from the crater. Miru fondled the piece of lava in his hands. One and different, he thought, the mountain and each rock on its face. The image of Kenetéa returned to his mind. Why had she implored him to come here? He lifted his eyes and looked toward the coast, where a line of breakers ringed the shore. One, many also, those waves and the ocean.

Miru listened. A bird cried above him. When it swept lower, he spotted the black wings and white breast of a sooty tern. Renghi's totem sister streaked past Miru, dipped sharply toward the lake, banked, planed and soared. He watched it, carefully, until its forked tail grew smaller and melted into the sunlight.

He sat on his cape. Miru breathed in and out. He heard a gust like the bird's flight, whirring wings that called back times with the people lost in them, floating on a breath of wind. He recollected tales of the beginnings, the founder and hero chiefs. Miru thought of his mother and father. He recalled old Te Rahai, who had taught him to sail and respect the ocean, to have a quiet heart. Will I ever have it again, he mused. He inhaled slowly and breathed out. Miru remembered the last rite of manhood in Marama's cave. He thought of Kuihi and Kuaha, the two lizards, and a smile fluttered over his lips. Miru recalled the voyage to Ragi, the sheltering tree, the goddesses who walked beneath it. He asked the air, Will those spirits come back to our island?

With his body still aching from the ordeal, the Ariki remembered their journey: Mohani, the little swallow who came and departed like a bird of passage; Renga Roiti, her young girl's smile, her new womanhood, her faith in him; the green island with its spreading tree, its graceful spirits; the calamity of the invaders, *Te Roku-o-witi* and their brave, twin-hulled canoe. Once again he recalled Kenetéa, her black eyes, her love for the earth, sea and sky. "*Ma Makemake*," he whispered, "*ma Tangaroa.*" He also invoked the goddesses of Ragi. He prayed for the saplings, the seeds that sprouted in the early rain, those that withered and died from drought, those that were stomped, hacked or torched by soldiers. He recalled the mother who was singing to her baby on her doorstep this afternoon, not far from where he sat on the mountain. Whether the child was alive or dead, Miru was certain—the woman cherished him. Could love be as strong as fear and death? More than anything now, he wanted to know.

Night fell on the island. The air chilled. Wrapping the cape around his shoulders, he lay down to sleep. Miru dreamed of the bird's flight and the memories it had brought back to him. When he awoke in the morning, he had made his decision.

He walked down the volcano's flank. Passing the ruined hut, he did not see the mother with her child's cradle at the threshold.

When Miru arrived in the square, he found Renga Roiti seated next to the dry well, scanning the sky. "I saw a sooty tern on Rano Raraku," he told her.

"That means the flock will come soon. She must have been a scout."

"Her flight told me what I have to do."

"What?" Renga Roiti appeared as open as daylight.

"The tern flew so high that I lost sight of her. I think she was telling me to strive for the unreachable." Miru paused to brace himself and Renghi for what he was about to say. "I'm going to enter the manbird contest at Orongo in the spring."

She let out a cry, and her eyes looked as round as coconuts. Feeling as though her heart were going to split open, Renga Roiti tried to speak; she could not move her tongue. The wind ruffled her red hair.

"You can teach me everything about the terns," Miru told her, "so I'd be the first to find the sacred egg."

She still could not find words. Renga Roiti gaped at Miru, her green eyes crossed by shadows.

"Will you teach me about your spirit birds?"

She struggled to answer. "Nuku—" was all she could say. That name stuck in Renghi's throat.

Miru touched the talisman around his neck; the whaletooth felt warm and smooth on his fingers. "Nuku can outswim me to the islet where the sooty terns roost," he admitted, "but he doesn't have you to teach him the birds' ways. Nobody on our island knows them as well as you—not even the other birds."

Miru poked his sister gently where her ribs showed. Renga Roiti did not laugh or smile. Breakers rumbled on the coast.

"Ru, people say you always seek—"Her voice cracked. "You always seek the impossible." Renghi paused. "First it was Kenetéa, then the mission, now—" Choking on her words again, she clutched her throat. Renga Roiti fixed her eyes on her brother, whose forehead was grooved with lines. She did not realize that her own brow was furrowed too.

"I need your help, Renghi."

"The sooty terns are my sisters," she said, trying to sound hopeful. "They guided us to Ragi, they helped us return to Vaitéa." She hesitated. At last she spurted, "Don't confront Nuku!" Her brother looked down. "Many of the men who swim in the strait are attacked by great-sharks," Renga Roiti said. "Even if you should make it to the islet where the terns mate, Nuku would find a way to hurt or kill you—I don't trust him. And let's imagine that somehow you beat him at Orongo, that you find the first egg, swim to Vaitéa without being struck by sharks and you become the new manbird. What then? How would you stop the killing?"

"Remember what Hiti told us in the palace?"

"What do you mean?"

"That the manbird has become almost as powerful as the king."

"Yes."

"So if I win the prize, I may be able to bring a truce and preserve the trees." Miru's stomach growled.

"Brother, how do you expect to win against Nuku if you're weak and hungry?"

"I'll be healthier again."

"You don't have time. Soon after the terns come back to Vaitéa, the priests will proclaim the birth of spring and the contest will start in a day or two." The young woman shuddered. "I'm scared, Ru."

Placing his arms on her frail shoulders, he said, "Be brave, Renghi. You're a woman." I'm the fearless one this time, Miru recognized.

She did not reply. For the only time in her life she did not have faith in her brother. Even on the worst days of the quest—during storms at sea, when their ship was scuttled on Ragi, when Mohani drowned, when she and Miru raved with thirst and hunger—she had never doubted him. Now Renghi could not imagine him or anyone besting Nuku. That mountain of a man won always—in war, swimming, love. She was afraid for her brother and their people. Yet she could not refuse his appeal.

Renga Roiti took his hand, turned and guided him to the terns' nesting ground. On the road they lingered to check their seedlings. Nearly all had withered or been lopped, crushed or set on fire. Only a handful of survivors had grown as high as Renghi's shins. She and Miru knelt, touched and spoke to the saplings, whose leaves had turned a deeper color than the green of first growth.

"Where have so many seeds and sprigs gone?" she asked him.

Miru did not answer. They walked through ashen fields. Sister and brother came to a ledge on the rocky coast, where they would wait for the sooty terns' arrival. They saw the offshore waters roiling with shoals of fish that drew the birds to Vaitéa each spring. Once the people had caught them from their boats with hooks or nets; now those schools were beyond the range of their ruined fleet.

On the third day's watch Renghi gripped Miru's arm. "Listen," she told him. He cocked one ear. He heard nothing except an onshore wind and rollers breaking on the rocks below. Fog swirled in the air.

"Ka-ara-ara!" she sang, imitating the terns' cry. "Te-vero-vero!" Miru distinguished those sounds, faintly. "Look!" called Renga Roiti. "Can you see them?" He surveyed the horizon.

"There!" she told him.

Miru detected dark points against the gray sky. As the flock came closer, their shapes grew, their calls became more distinct, then louder than the surf and breeze, drowning all other noises. Like a small girl Renghi jumped, echoing the birds' clatter: "Te-vero-vero! Ka-ara-ara!"

Those terns swept overhead, clouding the sky, veered and faced into the wind before landing on the rocky shelf.

When Renga Roiti saw her brother's head spattered with bird-droppings, she smiled. "That's the second time they've blessed you! You're the anointed one, Ru."

He picked up a strand of seaweed on the rocks and wiped his hair. "Renghi, have you ever considered why our tribes worship the sooty terns?"

"Because they're my spirit sisters?" She smiled again, seeing Miru's dark-brown hair still streaked with guano. Renga Roiti found more seaweed and helped her brother to clean his head.

"We live at the end of the world," Miru said, "too far away for anyone to reach us. But the terns come and go in freedom. They're our messengers from the outer world."

"They and the goddesses." Sister and brother looked at each other. It was the newest secret they shared.

Renghi showed Miru how to watch the terns, to know their habits, flights and calls, to listen, talk and sing to them. Few men or women possessed the skill of bird-speaking; later, when strangers landed on Vaitéa to snatch the people's souls, that knowledge was forgotten. Renga Roiti conveyed the rare language to her brother. How she loved to teach Miru!

In tidepools they hunted for oysters, clams, sea urchins and mussels. It saddened Ia's children to harvest those vanishing creatures. But they knew that Miru needed their strength inside him.

Renga Roiti sought the two old mariners, who fished the shallow waters and offered their sparse catch to her brother. Ihu gave his nephew the priest's allotment of taro and sweet potatoes. The family watched as

Miru's slight frame gathered a little flesh. They also noticed the changes in him—his air of loneliness, his unmoving gaze.

Each day he trained in the sea. He tried to recover his endurance and rhythmic stroke. In the bluewater he swam, dove, leapt and played with the dolphins.

For the first time since the days on Ragi, Miru began to feel calm. He was in his favorite place—on the shore, where the ocean, earth and wind meet. He was with Renga Roiti, close to his spirit brothers too, the dolphins. At the moment the war seemed far away. Only the memory of Koro and his father's humiliation, as well as the ghost of Kenetéa's hand, haunted his sleep.

When he walked close to the border, Raa troops scoffed at Miru. They reviled him for daring to enter the manbird contest. In some ways the Tuus were relieved that one of their tribesmen had volunteered to compete. But they also thought Miru was foolhardy to oppose the king's older son, the mightiest soldier and swimmer on Vaitéa. Who could defeat Nuku, they asked, that hill of a man, that unconquered soldier, heir to the throne?

Heedful of his purpose, Miru ignored them. Those men and women could not feel the ardor of his fury against the Raas—the soldiers who had killed and disgraced his father and many of his tribesmen, profaned their island, crushed and burned the seeds and shoots. Neither could those people grasp the allure of the unattainable.

After observing the flocks of terns and taking sightings of the sun, royal priests announced the first day of spring. The warlords and King Hiti declared a truce for the manbird rites.

Miru and his sister walked to the plain at Mataveri on a warm, cloudless day. Pilgrims were already celebrating the new season's birth. There he and Kenetéa had hidden behind the bushes years ago while the new manbird and the Raas heaped insults on his tribe. In the same spot she had offered her first moon-blood for peace on the island.

Ia's children watched men and women singing, dancing to the beat of calabash drums, rolling naked in the dirt. Priests of Makemake shook in rapture. Worshipers parted before the Ariki, who looked proud in his bearing at his sister's side.

Miru and Renga Roiti felt the sudden force of a wind blowing leaves in a gale: they saw Kenetéa's father, who was approaching with a cadre of Raa soldiers. Raunui wore a red cloak and a reed helmet topped with feathers. His body bristled with shields and weapons—a two-edged dagger in one hand, a great-shafted spear in the other, a sword at his waist, knives strapped to both arms. How could our tribe defeat an army of warriors like Raunui, Miru wondered, trembling.

That seasoned fighter stood in front of Koro's son, looking at him with a glare that would have turned many men to water. Miru shook, recalling when Mohani's father had appeared on the beach before the launching of their canoe. He could not remove his eyes from the tattoos of war clubs, crowned with human heads, that covered the soldier's arms.

"Tuu!" the man called, his nostrils flaring. "This time you cannot escape over the sea." Raunui rocked on the balls of his feet, waving his knife, ready to brawl. Like the ropes of a ship the veins bulged on his neck. It was then that Miru noticed the warrior's wife, doleful Neira, cowering beyond the Raa troops.

He ordered Renga Roiti to leave. She joined the people who had formed a silent ring around her brother and Raunui. Flies droned in the heat.

"Miru!" Kenetéa's father shouted, bobbing on his toes, looking big as a tree. Raunui no longer favored his leg with the sinuous white scar. "You kidnapped my son and let him die at sea. You've sneaked onto our lands like a coward again. You've been with my daughter and my wife. Now I must kill you."

Raunui spoke these words as if they were nothing. The Raas murmured and closed ranks around their tribesman. Where were Tuu soldiers when the Ariki needed them?

The air laid eggs of perspiration on Miru's brow. His nostrils quivered, and his mouth felt dry. His body wavered. As Koro had taught him, he inhaled deeply, trying to compose himself, to keep his head clear.

Miru stared into the warrior's eyes, black like Kenetéa's but surrounded by tattooed coils and spirals. "Raunui," he started, "your son's a hero. Someday our tribes will tell stories about Mohani. Without his starsongs we would—" Miru stopped. From the glower on the soldier's face he knew those words meant nothing to Raunui; they were like a bird's feathers blown on the wind.

The warrior unstrapped a dagger from his right arm and pointed it at Miru's heart. "Draw your knife," he said.

Miru glanced at Neira, who was sobbing and shrinking behind her husband. "I have no reason to fight you," he told Raunui.

"You have the best reason of all—I killed your father."

Renga Roiti saw her brother's back stiffen: he appeared suddenly larger, swollen with rage. Miru ground his teeth and clenched both fists while blood pounded in his ears.

"Koro made good long-pig!" Raunui blared. "We cut off his head, roasted and ate his body." The soldier placed the tip of his dagger against his gums. "Your father's flesh sticks between my teeth. For the last course we sucked the marrow from his bones." Raunui made a slurping sound. The Raa troops broke into laughter.

Deep inside of Miru something surged, thick and heavy. It gushed out in a throaty cry as he drew his knife and leaped. Raunui sprang away, brandishing his sword in one hand and his dagger in the other, opened his mouth and released a bellow that raised the hair on the people's arms. That warrior hurtled toward his enemy, who felt a gust of wind on his face and body. Raunui swung with the knife and missed, made a back-swipe and caught Miru's right leg, where blood spouted from the thigh. The young man felt moist heat on his slashed limb.

As Miru recovered, Raunui thrust his sword again. Koro's son dodged the soldier's lunge. While his rival continued moving forward, he reached and drove his dagger into the side of the man's neck, where the obsidian blade crunched and made a hollow sound, slicing through flesh, muscle and sinew before cleaving there. Raunui gagged, tried to extract the knife, coughed: blood spurted from his mouth, nose and ears. He staggered and fell backward with a thump on the ground, making a burst of dust. His legs jerked. Death slackened the warrior's jaw while his vacant eyes reflected a passing cloud. Beneath Raunui's hair a dark, red stream flowed, mingling with a pool of blood spilled from Miru's thigh.

Swift as a tern Renga Roiti dashed to her brother. She tore a strip of tapa from her waistcloth and tied it above the gash on his leg. With another piece she plugged the wound. Both she and Miru must have recalled the day when he had treated Mohani's shark bites, using a tourniquet to stanch the bleeding.

The Ariki knelt over Raunui. He withdrew his knife from the soldier's neck. Then he plunged the obsidian blade into the dry soil, pulled it free and wiped it on the tapa cloth around his wounded leg, stained now with Raunui's blood as well as his own. In the sunlight his weapon flashed. Koro's words from long ago resounded in Miru's head: "One day you'll thrust this knife to avenge your uncles' deaths." My father's too, he thought.

Neira emerged from the crowd. The agony on her face silenced everyone, Raas and Tuus. She stepped into the circle of men around the corpse.

Kenetéa's mother kneeled over her fallen husband. "*Aûé! Aûé!* Raunui!" she cried. "If only I could be the earth that drinks your blood." She dropped to her knees and licked the damp soil by the warrior's head.

Standing slowly, Neira wrung her hands, lifting them toward the sky. She looked first at Miru, then the crowd and shrieked, "*Aûé!* A curse on war and on both tribes!" She collapsed onto Raunui's chest.

The bystanders trained their eyes on Miru. He placed his dagger in the sheath on his arm. Grimacing with pain, pressing his thigh with one hand to stem the bleeding, he limped away. Renga Roiti followed. Her toes stepped on scarlet drops that trickled from her brother's leg.

When they were alone by the shore, Miru halted. "Sister," he said in a faraway voice, "think of Mohani and Kenetéa—I've murdered their father in front of Neira." Tears coursed from his eyes, making narrow rivulets through the dust on his face and neck.

With her small arms Renghi embraced him. She felt the warm blood from his thigh, soaking through the band around his wound, spotting her waistcloth. "Ru, maybe this was the decisive battle—the one Marama told you to fight. Maybe this is the end."

He gazed into the distance, remembering the priestess. "No," he said. Trying to move, he groaned, seized his right leg with both hands, slumped and dropped to his knees. Renga Roiti assisted her brother to his feet, bearing most of his weight, helping him to walk. Now she was the stronger of the two.

When they reached their great-house, Miru asked her to go inside. As soon as she crossed the threshold, he sagged to the ground, retched and vomited. He crawled closer to the door, laid down his head, closed his eyes. Miru fell into a bottomless sleep.

When he awoke, he was lying on his back in the longroom. The *ao* stood next to him at the hearth, weather-bitten, upended in the ashes. Miru felt heartsore and weary, worn like the old paddle. Above him the shapes of Ia, her brother Ihu and red-haired Renga Roiti appeared like figures in a dream, looking into his face.

Miru held up his left palm. He tried to speak, but his voice did not come, as though it had drained from his body with the blood. "Killing hand," he managed to say finally, looking pale and wild.

Koro's widow leaned over her son. She hugged him and caressed his dark-brown braids, still coated with dirt. Ia's eyes were bloodshot from weeping. "Your father wanted you to be a soldier," she said. "He's had his way at last."

When the mother loosened her embrace, the priest spoke. "Ariki, your sister told us how Raunui taunted you at Mataveri. He uttered the gravest insult and professed his guilt for your father's death and dishonor." Ihu's voice grew louder and his nose, pointed as a bowsprit, turned red. "You had no choice. If you had not reacted with force, that warrior would have slain you. And our people would have been despised and rejected."

Staring at both of his palms, Miru said, "I have bloody hands like a warlord. I've failed to break the circle of death. I've murdered Mohani's and Kenetéa's father."

"Forget the Raa girl!" Ihu called. He struck the earthen floor with his staff of sandalwood.

I cannot forget her, Miru thought without the strength to answer his uncle, knowing that he had lost Kenetéa's love forever.

"Your sister told me that Raunui's widow cursed both tribes and the war," the tall priest resumed. "That woman's mad—Neira doesn't know the time for peace has gone." Ihu swept a long arm in the air. "We have to resist the Raas or die." Miru recalled Marama's warning in the cave.

The priest placed a hand on his nephew's shoulder. Miru saw the white hairs that flecked Ihu's beard. "There's more," his uncle said. "At noon today we received a message from our burial ground. The Raas have broken the necks of our Living Faces, toppled them, gouged their whaletooth eyes and defaced our ancestors' tombs. Our bereavement and our hunger for revenge is sharper now."

Miru burned till dawn with fever, for two more days and nights, calling out Kenetéa's and her father's names. At dusk and dawn the sun spread blood in the sky. Ia and Renga Roiti sobbed as they treated the injury on the Ariki's thigh. Knowing what lay ahead of him, gods, goddesses and spirits wept too.

Chapter 12

Sacred Egg

The absence of rain forced Miru to bathe in the surf. As he had done for several days now, he cleansed his knife-cut, wiping it with seaweed. It had healed around the edges but still oozed blood and pus.

He dried himself in the dawn light. At the house Ihu anointed his nephew's body with oil, placed a belt of tree bark around the young Ariki's waist and a straw-colored cape on his shoulders, one that had belonged to Koro. For luck Miru wore his grandfather's whalebone amulet.

The family met around *Te Roku-o-witi* in the longroom. The tall priest raised his arms and blessed his nephew in the name of Tangaroa, the Tuus' god of oceans, whose face adorned the paddle on the hearth. Next the priest did something that astonished everyone: he invoked Makemake, the Raas' lord of earth. The gods are changing, Miru said to himself. He traded glances with Renga Roiti. She understood. Brother and sister embraced.

Ia gave Miru her blessing: "May the spirits also help you." He looked into his mother's eyes. She too knows about those gods and goddesses, he thought, the spirits of the woods, wind and sea. Once more he and his sister exchanged looks.

Miru hobbled from the house as the sun tipped above the world. I killed her father, he thought—now I'm the one who limps. Ihu and Renga

169

Roiti followed. Miru kept his eyes on the ground. He did not want to see the blood that stained the eastern sky.

They reached the field of Mataveri, where the king had declared a truce for the manbird rites. From all corners of Vaitéa leaders had assembled with survivors of their clans. Many more had died in the wars, from disease, hunger or distress. A few milled around the site where Miru had fought Raunui, the soil that swallowed the warrior's blood.

Raa soldiers spit on the ground when Koro's son passed. He did not pay attention to them or to the men and women with faces dyed red or yellow, with their crowns of feathers, nor to those who danced naked in circles, the rongorongo singers with their deep-voiced chants, the sorcerers with their cries and shrieks. Without averting his eyes he led his uncle and sister up the flank of Rano Kau, beyond its sunken crater to the ceremonial grounds.

On the volcano's far side the king, priests and nobles waited on a platform overlooking the sea. Ranks of warriors surrounded them. When they sighted Miru, a pair of musicians blew conch horns.

All waited for the king's son. In a sweeping red cloak he strode up the hill ahead of his tribesmen. Nuku's presence imposed a hush on the crowd.

Then the musicians blared the conch shells louder. Blind Hiti lowered himself onto his carved throne. He invoked Makemake, god of earth and the sooty tern.

With solemn steps, ushered by two aged priests, a pair of white virgins advanced. Miru felt a sudden joy. Those young women had come straight from Ana o Keke, where they had lived in the cavern with Kenetéa, seen her skin the color of moonlight. He smiled at them. The corners of their lips curved upward, and their eyes flashed; except for the priests, those girls had not seen a man for months or years. Meanwhile Nuku watched the sea below.

The contestants removed their capes and let them fall to the ground. Both Miru and the prince had a knife of obsidian lashed to one arm. The virgins handed each of the men a reed basket containing a small gourd of water, compact bunches of dried bananas and sweet potatoes. The Ariki and Nuku strapped them to one shoulder. Following usage in the time of kings, they opened their baskets for the girls to place a headband inside, woven of fine tapa cloth, with a pouch at the center. There one of the two men, the victor, would safeguard the egg.

The two girls mounted fire-rocks that were incised with images of virgins and menbird. Both faced the ocean; the priests knelt before them. With a stone chisel those men began to etch pictures of the girls' grooves on the rocks.

King Hiti lifted his bulk from the throne. "Nuku of the mountain!" he piped. "Miru of the dolphins! Every spring our two peoples come together at Orongo to celebrate the sooty terns' arrival. The truce between tribes will hold until our rituals have ended." Hiti paused to catch his breath. "One of you will be chosen to retrieve the first egg—each year it brings renewal to our island. Already the priests are cutting figures of virgins into the rocks to make our women fruitful."

The king raised a plump arm and pointed to the sea. "At the signal you must climb down the bluff and swim across the strait to the islet of Motu Nui. There you must seek the egg of a sooty tern. The one who finds it first must swim back to Vaitéa with his opponent behind him, scale the cliff and put the sacred prize in my hand. He will be named manbird and life will flourish for another year on our island." The king paused again. As though he could see them with his blank eyes, he looked toward his son and Miru. "If either of you attempts to harm the other, he shall be hurled over the bluff to his death. And his rival shall be named the winner."

The contestants faced one another. Eager for action, Nuku rubbed his limbs, whose muscles strained and bulged. Each of his arms had the might of two men. Miru took long breaths to calm himself. Some animal thing moved in his frame, something old, keeping him alert and poised.

He and Nuku crouched for the start. Ia's son winced from the tenderness in his right leg. Over the palisades they saw the three islets: a pointed crag, closest to shore; a flat surface beyond it; finally broad Motu Nui, the terns' home. All were surrounded by jagged rocks where waves beat and spewed foam.

A deep-chested man sounded *Rapa Nui*, the conch blown twice a year for ages. Its blast filled the air and echoed from the fire-rocks. The crowd cheered. Musicians played.

Nuku dashed to the cliff's edge. Turning his back to the sea, he dropped over the rim and descended the sheer escarpment, grasping for holds on the rock-face. Miru tottered behind the prince. Each time he lowered his bad leg, he could feel a throb where Raunui's dagger had slit his thigh.

Before he was halfway down the precipice, the warlord landed on the stony beach. Nuku charged into the surf, plunged beneath a breaker, emerged on the far side, stroked around the rocks and pulled forward with his huge arms. His feet churned a spuming wake.

Miru fell to the beach on his good leg. When his right foot hit the stones, he felt a twinge that made him stagger. He caught his balance, inhaled slowly as Koro had taught him, pivoted and stumbled into the surf.

The cold water covered Miru's thighs and soothed his lesion. He dove under a curling wave, surfaced, paddled around the rocks, unhurried, pacing himself. Far ahead he saw the plume of Nuku's kick. Dancing and jumping, people shouted from the palisades. The two opponents heard those voices recede behind them.

As he swam across the channel, Miru felt his bad leg weaken. He feared that blood flowing from his thigh would draw great-sharks. He drifted by the first islet, too far from its shore, recalling how *Mahina-i-te-pua* had cut a crooked path on the voyage home, veering farther and farther off course.

By now Nuku had swum out of sight. The red sun dipped in the sky. Miru tried to keep his gaze from the blood that smeared clouds on the horizon. He felt pangs in his leg, stabbing up and down. Ahead of him he saw the level outline of the second crag where it rose above the water in the waning light.

Miru could not withstand the current that was driving him toward the rocks. Rather than swim against the tide, he waited for a roller to rise, and he settled into its curve. The wave broke, sweeping him to the islet's seaward side. As it pushed him beyond the tip of land, he raked over submerged boulders that gouged his chest, stomach and limbs.

Flailing in the death-light, Miru fought to stay afloat. His dagger-wound and the fresh cuts smarted. Cramps shot through him. The new gashes and the old injury on his thigh seeped blood. Miru's body hurt from his feet to his braided hair.

Gulping water and choking, he sent silent appeals to the gods, goddesses and spirits. He touched the *reimiro* on his neck, sputtered Koro's and Te Rahai's names. The last thing Miru remembered was a thin, scarlet, dripping moon in the sky.

When he awoke, he was lying faceup on a beach, gasping like a beached dolphin, his legs splayed. Miru did not know where he was, how he had gotten there. Have Tangaroa's tides washed me ashore, he wondered. Did the gods and graceful spirits guide me across the channel? Did my totem brothers lead me, shooting water from their blowholes, shielding me from sharks? He imagined Marama, standing on the sea cliffs at Kote Pora with her white robe swirling in the breeze: did the priestess somehow rescue me, he asked the air and ocean, so that I would fulfill her prophecies? He dropped into a profound sleep again.

The prince found his rival on the beach of Motu Nui, lying helpless on his back. Nuku carried the limp body to a large grotto where he had taken shelter.

Miru retched saltwater and raved with fever. The king's son lay close by, confident that he would be the new manbird, satisfied that he had delivered the man who once saved his brother from drowning. Nuku fell asleep and snored in the dank air. At dawn he left the cavern to survey the terns' home.

When Miru woke, trickling sweat, his body quaked. His eyes opened and blinked; he saw nothing in the blackness. At first he thought he had been carried to sea by the surf, that he had drowned, sunk to the ocean floor. But the throb in his right leg told him that he must be alive. As if he were touching a friend's hand, Miru caressed the scalding wound on his thigh. His mouth felt parched. He craved sweet water to wet his throat and cool his flesh. Groaning with pain and thirst, he twitched on the cave floor. Miru fell into a sleep of the dead.

He awoke with chills. Beads of perspiration covered his body. Miru moaned and shivered.

"Ho!" a husky voice called.

In the darkness Nuku approached. He extracted the gourd from the reed basket on his arm, filled with precious rainwater, to moisten Miru's hair, face, neck and shoulders. Lifting the Ariki's head with one hand, Nuku gave him to drink with the other.

"Where are we?" Miru asked. His voice did not sound like his own.

"On Motu Nui. The tides must have washed you onto the beach."

"When?"

"Two nights ago."

"Why didn't you leave me there to die?"

"You rescued my brother from the sea—I've done the same for you. Now I owe you nothing." Nuku paused. "Besides it wouldn't be a challenge for me to retrieve the egg without a rival."

"Have you found it?" Waiting for the prince's reply, Miru held his breath. His teeth chattered.

Nuku did not rush to answer. "No. But I will find it. First I want you to recover because the best contender wants a worthy opponent." He paused. "By the way I tried to make a fire but it wouldn't kindle—that's a servant's chore in the royal sanctuary." Nuku's laugh resounded through the cave. "While you were asleep I filled the gourd in your basket with rainwater and placed some food inside. That's the last aid I can give you, Ariki." The king's son turned and walked into the darkness.

Remembering the boat-shaped talisman, Miru felt around his neck; the amulet had not been lost in the channel. He groped for the dagger, still strapped to his arm. Next Miru reached for food inside the virgins' basket. He removed drenched bananas and sweet potatoes, rubbed them and squeezed out as much moisture as his weak hands allowed.

He clasped the gourd, pulled out its tapa plug, raised it above his head. He opened his mouth to let the water drip onto his tongue and throat. Unable to swallow, Miru gagged. He poured the fluid over his cuts and knife-wound.

By the third night he could drink a few drops and nibble on the paste of bananas and sweet potatoes. Nuku has helped me to survive, Miru admitted, so that I can be a witness to his triumph. He had a glimpse of days without light or hope—the cavern, the stone floor, the damp, stale air. He understood part of what Kenetéa had to endure in the white virgins' cave.

Miru spent two more nights in the darkness. His body continued to shake with fever. On the sixth day from their crossing he finished his stores of food and water. He longed to see the sun and sky, to breathe fresh air, to feel wind on his face.

He placed his empty gourd in the basket. He lashed the straw vessel to his arm. Following the echo of surf, Miru wriggled over the stone floor until he found the cave mouth. After so many black days the sun dazzled him. He said a prayer to the gods, the goddesses and spirits of the wind, woods and sea.

Miru attempted to rise. He sank to the ground. Like a baby on all fours he clambered toward the sea, rasping his trunk and limbs on the pebbled beach. He toppled into the shallows. The sea salt stung his wounds. Squinting at the sky, he rolled onto his back. Miru was thankful to be in the light again, on the shoreline where land, air and ocean meet.

He clawed his way along the beach. He hunted for seaweed and ate the stems, bulbs and leaves. Miru squirmed onto a ledge where rain had formed little pools, reflecting sun, sky and clouds on their surface. He wondered if it had even sprinkled on Vaitéa, where the water would have nourished their saplings. Remembering the dogs that used to thrive on his island, he lapped with his tongue, grateful that he could swallow. He scooped and filled his small gourd with rainwater.

Next he foraged dry kelp and driftwood. He stuck them in the virgins' basket and the bark belt around his waist. Miru dragged himself to the cavern with his load. Before entering, he stopped to listen. Between the crashing of waves he could hear it: "Ka-ara-ara! Te vero-vero!" He thought of his sister, how happy she would be to hear the cries of her totem spirits. He also realized how much he had grown used to Renghi, how much she had helped him, how lonely he felt without her. What if Nuku already has the first egg in his possession, he worried.

Like a hurt animal he crawled into the cave. Miru placed his belt of tree-bark and his basket with the gourd on the ground. He lit a fire to dry himself by the flames, banked the wood and lay down to sleep.

When he awakened, he touched his forehead; for the first time on Motu Nui the fever did not burn his hand. The chills had gone, but the knife-cut still gnawed Miru's right leg. He ached and bled where the rocks had chafed him.

He strove toward the light again. Miru reached the cavern's mouth and slivered to the beach. Through red clouds he saw the sun rising. For the second time he washed his wounds in the surf.

Listening for the birds, Miru limped along the coast. He heard them faintly. As he walked slowly in their direction, the calls grew louder. He shinnied up a ledge, where he viewed a colony of sooty terns, hundreds of them on a ridge that overlooked the sea.

The breeding ground stank of guano and shrilled with the birds' cries. On one side Nuku stood, reaching for a group of terns, who startled and flew off. When the prince caught sight of his rival, he glowered at him as though Koro's son were an intruder. With a gesture of scorn the warrior turned his back. He hasn't found the egg, Miru thought.

The terns raised an uproar with their calls. Females roosted while males hovered around them. The air reeked of bird-dung.

Keeping an eye on Nuku, the Ariki moved over sheets of guano. He spoke to the terns in a soft voice and hummed the songs that Renga Roiti had taught him. At first the birds fled. By dusk they had grown used to him. Nuku followed his contender, watching and learning.

Miru knelt by a female tern. With eyes set in a dark band around her head, she gazed at him. They're my sister's eyes, he said in a whisper, green like Mother's and mine too, like the cove of Anakena. How he missed Renghi! From the lessons she had taught him, he knew that this hen, with her swollen breast, must be close to hatching.

Miru returned to his cavern and built a fire against the moisture of the night. He imagined the king's son in a clammy grotto without light or heat.

The next day he passed Nuku on the coast. Chewing a raw fish, the soldier sat on a rock, sunning himself. The prince must have made his catch by hand, beyond the surf, Miru guessed, aware that he lacked the strength to do the same himself. The fish's bones and entrails formed a pile at the warrior's feet. Nuku grinned as Ia's son tramped along the shore, looking like a ghost.

At dawn a storm arrived, covering the islet with clouds, making the skies weep. Miru thanked Hiro for his tears, hoping they had fallen on the withered shoots and seedlings too. He scoured for tinder before the showers could soak it. When he entered the cave, his stack of driftwood had disappeared. Either Nuku has learned to make a fire, he calculated, or he's snatching my fuel from spite.

On the next day the wind began to howl. The king's son and Miru could hardly keep their footing on the storm-swept mating ground. Both men were sopped from cloudbursts. With mucus dribbling from his nose, with bloodshot eyes, coughing and sneezing, Nuku was sick. He scowled at his challenger, who appeared gaunt in the rain. Miru returned the soldier's look. In Nuku's eyes he recollected the wrath he had seen in Raunui's glare.

He lit a pair of fires that evening, one near the grotto's mouth, the other deep in its belly. Between the two he rested with one eye open. Miru could not forget the hatred in the prince's stare.

He heard footfalls in the night. When he raised his head to look, Miru made out a shadow looming on the cave wall. He drew his knife and clenched it. His muscles were taught like a boat's rigging at full sail. Miru braced himself to spring, as well as a man could leap with mangled legs. Beads of sweat lined his upper lip.

Against the glow of the fire he saw Nuku skulking toward him, holding a double-edged dagger whose blade flashed in the embers' gleam. The king's son prowled closer to where his rival lay on the cavern floor. As he listened to the warrior's breathing, Miru's mouth was dry, and blood beat in his ears.

He bounded to his feet and alighted in front of Nuku. Through the slits of his eyes the soldier looked down at him. He swiped with the dagger and struck Miru's belly, where blood spurted, spraying the fire and making the coals hiss. Nuku lunged at his foe, who shifted to one side; the prince's body pitched onto the cave floor, landing by the blaze with a thump. Miru dropped his knife, scooped glowing embers and shoved them onto the warrior's thighs. Nuku released a yell that reverberated against the cavern walls. Trying to quench the coals on his legs, he twisted on the ground, over and over, while Koro's son kneaded his hands to soothe their charred palms. Blood dripped from Miru's stomach. With a burnt hand he picked up his dagger.

Nuku rolled beyond the outer fire. Holding his lacerated stomach with one hand, his knife in the other, Miru followed. Wind gusted, and rain slanted into the cavern's mouth.

Miru stooped over his opponent. Nuku attempted to rise but collapsed on the stony beach. When he tried again, Ia's son gave him a feeble tug, barely enough to help the soldier gain his feet.

"Nuku, that's the last aid I can give you." Those were the final words that Miru would utter to the prince on the islet. He did not want to waste more breath on that warlord.

Sneering at his rival, Nuku licked the blood off his dagger. He turned and lumbered toward his grotto.

Miru reeled to the shore, where he slumped onto his knees in the surf. He splashed himself. The seawater cooled his seared palms, the scrapes on his arms and legs, the new cut on his belly.

He strained to stand. He wobbled to his cave and reached the inner fire. Thinking about Nuku and the day to come, he lay down, but he could not rest.

By dawn the storm had passed. With sleepless eyes Miru slouched to the coast, hunting for strands of seaweed. He stuffed them into his fresh wound. His hands were singed and swollen where he had grasped the embers.

In the afternoon Miru groveled toward the terns' nesting place. Nuku shambled behind him and stalked his contender around the roost. The king's son grimaced from the pain of his burns. Keeping an eye on the prince, Miru unsheathed his dagger.

Ever more thickly the terns were clustering, crying, wheeling. Their calls grew strident. Shrinking from the keen sounds, Miru and the soldier packed their ears with shreds of tapa from their headbands. In the east a round moon rose through flame-red clouds. Evening folded her wings over Motu Nui.

The Ariki perched on the rocky shelf, clutching his stomach with scorched hands, keeping vigil. Nuku sat on the opposite side of the ledge, waiting. The terns had ceased their clamor for the night; only a few squeaked and croaked. Miru breathed in the stench of bird-dung.

Then he heard it—the odd cry Renghi had imitated for him—low and pierced with yearning. He spotted a nearby female who was making the haunting sound. Miru checked for the warlord, who was looking away, kneading the welts on his thighs.

In the moonlight he listed over slimy guano toward the hen. He crouched, talking to her in a hushed voice so that Nuku could not hear, making Renga Roiti's soft music. Miru extended his arm and grazed the tern's breast—whiter than our canoe's foam-flower, he thought—caressed it, soothing the bird, moving his hand over the downy feathers. On his fingertips he could feel her breast fluttering from the sound that was singing through her body.

On a downward stroke of his hand Miru brushed the egg, warm and moist. Murmuring one of Renga Roiti's songs, he made a silent prayer to the gods and spirits, placed his fingers around the sphere and let it roll into his palm.

It lay in his hand, perfect as the moon in the sky. He observed the egg, darker than those he had seen in the past: pearl-gray, speckled with ruddy spots. Asking the bird to pardon him for taking her fruit, he straightened and eased backward, still watching her, humming. From the corner of one eye he saw Nuku squatting among terns.

Miru scrambled up the highest rock on the islet. At the top he stood on his scarred legs and gazed toward Vaitéa; against the moonlit sky he sighted the palisades of Orongo. He caught his breath, filled his lungs with air, felt a pang in his stomach, lifted his voice and sent the manbird's shout across the strait: "Miru of the dolphins!"

He watched the coast. Soon he heard a blast of *Rapa Nui,* the conch shell that would not sound again for a year. A signal fire blazed on the sea cliff. The Ariki knew his cry of hurt and exultation had reached the islanders.

Nuku also heard the shell's blare. From his lungs he let out a roar that made the terns scatter: "*Aûé aûé aûé!*" He understood the meaning of Miru's call.

With the egg in his hand the Ariki moved as if he were in a dream. He entered the cave. From his reed basket he pulled the headband with its pouch of woven tapa. Miru limped to the shore, where he submerged the sooty tern's egg in the sea, placed it snugly in the headband's pocket and tied it to his brow.

He slipped into the moon-glossed surf with Nuku close behind him. The saltwater bit his raw hands, the wound on his thigh and the fresh cut on his belly. Turning his head, he saw the king's son standing in shallow water with tears glistening on his face. It was the only time that Nuku was known to weep.

Miru's palms and the knife-cut festered. Once more he feared that sharks would catch the scent of his blood. His body was weak and crippled.

With the egg strapped to his forehead, he swam over the slippery path of death. At his back he heard and felt the thrust of Nuku's strokes. Paddling through heavy seas, Miru remembered his father, his grandfather, their fallen tribesmen. He thought of the seeds and shoots, the delicate saplings that took root on their island, those the Raas downed or set on fire. He drew strength from his anger, from grief and love for his dead—for Te Rahai and Koro—for the living—Ia, his sister, white-armed Kenetéa.

The moon crossed the sky as the two men moved over the strait. They passed the flat rock, then the pointed islet. As tides towed them closer to Vaitéa, they saw bonfires at Orongo. They heard voices, muffled by the sounds of the sea, and they saw blurred figures on the cliff tops.

A wave cast Miru onto the land, where he belched water and seaweed. His chest, stomach, arms and thighs bled where he had grated them on hidden rocks. The blisters on his hands stung, the slash on his belly and the lesion on his thigh pulsed. Miru felt for the egg on his forehead. It was there, smooth and whole.

Nuku floated onto the shore like a beached whale. Panting, spitting seawater, Miru said a prayer of gratitude for their safety and the egg's. Neither he nor his contender had drowned, been dashed to death on crags or struck by great-sharks. The two swimmers crumpled onto the stony strand.

The moon dropped into the sea. When a red dawn broke, the men stirred. Ia's son and Nuku floundered to their feet and shuffled toward the cliff.

Miru began to climb. As he scrabbled up the escarpment, he did not look behind him at the prince. The burns on his hands bled. His cuts throbbed.

When he attained the cliff edge, a new sun spread its light on the world. Gripping the rock, he tugged himself over the rim, chafing his chest, stomach and legs. Conch horns blasted, players danced on drums, people lifted their voices in song.

Miru trudged to the platform where Hiti sat on his throne, surrounded by priests and nobles. The Ariki gulped for air. He sagged to his knees. Sluggishly he stood and plodded forward to place the egg in the king's fat palm. When Hiti felt it, he sniveled like a boy.

Nuku approached the throne. He scanned the audience, set his teeth and puffed out his chest, as if preparing a speech. "Father," he announced, almost out of breath. "I was the one who found the first egg on Motu Nui. But," he said, raising his voice, spinning and pointing at his rival, "this Tuu snatched it from me and crossed the strait before I could catch him."

Miru was astonished to see the prince lie without a sign of remorse or doubt on his face, wearing a mask of offended righteousness. "Describe the egg," he told Nuku, breathless, standing in front of the soldier to obstruct his view of the small sphere enfolded in Hiti's hand.

"It's white of course, like the foam of a breaking wave."

The king ordered a priest and a noble to examine the egg. After they had whispered in his ear, Hiti held it up for everyone to see. "Nuku," he said, "you've shamed your father and your tribe not because you lost the contest, but because you've tried to win by deception. This tern's egg is gray like the inside of an oyster shell, marked with spots the color of dried blood." The king turned to Miru with tears welling in his eyes: "Son of Koro, in time you may choose the penalty that Nuku deserves." Hiti scowled at his son, who skulked away, skirting the crowd.

The people murmured until a priest heralded the winner: "Ariki!"

Staring at the sea with round eyes, Miru pronounced the manbird's call in a quavering voice. "*Vai Riva*, Calm Water," he divulged, "will be the name of the year in which I serve." For the first time since he had touched land, Miru realized that he was truly awake, that he was not dreaming or raving. He felt a shudder of elation.

Healers cleansed the manbird's bleeding palms and belly. With a honed blade the priests shaved Miru's dark-brown hair, lashes and eyebrows, painted his face crimson and white with the god's wide-open eyes. They covered his scalp with a wreath of lustrous female tresses, black, red and brown. They tethered the wooden figure of Makemake to his back, with its head of a bird, its body of a man.

As the priests adorned him, Miru stole a glance of Renga Roiti in the crowd. Her smile beamed from ear to ear. Seeing her next to their mother and Ihu, he knew that he was home. For a moment Miru thought he could feel Koro's presence.

Ia walked forward to meet her son. "If only your father could be with us," she said in a voice like water, one that he had not heard for so long. She placed Koro's yellow cape on her son's heaving shoulders.

"I sensed him here," Miru said. She smiled sadly. Ia fondled her son's shaved head, bare as her own, and rejoined the crowd.

With tears spilling from his blank eyes, Hiti returned the pearl-colored treasure to the victor. "Do not be harsh with my son and our tribe, Ariki," the blind ruler pleaded in a whimper. Miru was shocked to hear the king acknowledge his title.

The new manbird took the egg in both of his sore, burnt palms, cupping it there. He did not tell Hiti that his son had assaulted him in the cave—a breach that would have brought Nuku's death. For now he would keep his opponent's crime to himself and withhold punishment for his deceit. After all, Miru accepted, the prince had saved his life on Motu Nui.

Rongorongo singers chanted hymns to the manbird. Childless women rubbed their bellies against the images that the priests had carved into the rocks. Tuu lords and their people danced, vaulted, reveled on the grass.

Raas wailed, pulled their hair and slit their arms and legs with fishbone daggers, smearing their robes with blood.

One by one the warlords presented themselves to Miru, pledging their oaths to obey him. "Prepare a stack of kindling," he instructed those men.

When they had done it, Miru commanded: "Lay down your shields, clubs, knives and spears." Jolted by his defeat of Nuku and the warrior's disgrace, in the first flush of devotion, the warriors complied. Nobody would have opposed a man who held the god's egg in his hand.

Once the soldiers had deposited their war-gear, Miru called for silence. Lifting the egg, with a pang in his belly, he stated in a voice that seemed to come from far away: "Here the killing ends." He instructed Engo and Nuku, lords of their clans, to kindle the towering heap of weapons.

"Maybe you'll learn to light a fire now," Miru told the prince. The dawn of a bitter smile fleeted over Nuku's face.

The two warlords kindled the pile. Priests raised Miru onto a wooden litter. As they carried him away, the hill of weapons smoldered and caught fire. For a few moments it turned the night into day. It would burn until sunrise, billowing dark smoke, consuming wooden hafts, rods, and hilts, melting knife blades and spearheads down to blackened stone, cinders and ashes.

Priests and pilgrims carried Miru to the foot of Rano Kau. They screamed, leapt and writhed in the sun, their bodies shaking before the big-eyed god and his anointed one. When the procession reached the plain at Mataveri, the people danced, romped and devoured foods baked in earth-ovens for this day—yams, taro, sweet potatoes, mussels, eels, lobsters. The tumult grew, laughter echoed on the fire-rocks, and many islanders rejoiced. Others would never drive the acrimony from their hearts.

Among the crowd Miru spotted the woman whose lullaby he had heard on the volcano's slope. She looked grave and no longer held a small cradle in her arms. Has she lost her child to famine or the wars, he fretted, like so many mothers? Again he asked himself if love could be as strong as fear, hatred and death. How, when will I learn, he pondered.

In the morning priests and pilgrims bore him to the crater of Rano Kau. In accordance with age-old rites the manbird punctured the egg lightly at both ends with the point of his dagger, cautious to avoid splitting the shell. He blew half of its yolk into the lake. Then the men conveyed him to the second volcano, Rano Raraku, the sacred mountain where Kenetéa had entreated him to go, where Miru had sighted the first sooty tern of spring. He blew the egg's other half into the reedy eye of water.

The group wound up the crater's flank, descended the far side and reached a slope overlooking the sea. There Miru entered the manbird's house, whitewashed and bleached by the sun, bordered by taboo stones. After the priests had swabbed his cuts and burns, they departed.

With woven tapa he filled the eggshell. Miru hung it from the highest beam in the house. When rays of the setting sun sliced through the door, he noticed a thin crack in the shell. "Vaitéa and my people are as fragile as this egg," he said in a soft voice, caressing the smooth sphere.

Each morning runners arrived with herbs, kelp and saltwater to treat his wounds. They did not stay long. Miru prayed, brooded and felt his loneliness, the gods and goddesses inside. Finally that great heart rested.

Chapter 13

Vai Riva

Soon the royal *maoris* etched a tattoo of the large-eyed god between the dolphins on Miru's chest. It was the manbird's sign, the emblem of his authority. The incisions bled and burned. On Miru's belly the knife-slash still wept blood. The wound on his thigh, where Raunui had cut him, closed at last.

He walked like a person in a trance. His eyes were round and did not move in their gaze. A few islanders claimed he was possessed by Makemake, the god whose figure hung on his back and peered from his chest. But with Renga Roiti he was almost his old self, a big brother who somehow had beaten Nuku, who was the new manbird, who might become the most powerful man on Vaitéa.

Many felt the force of Miru's mana. Some were wary and resented him. His troubles were not over.

To the whitewashed house he called the warlords, who considered themselves fortunate to cross the threshold once forbidden by taboo. Those seasoned killers admired the only man who had ever thwarted Nuku. Standing beneath the gray, spotted egg on the roof-beam, Miru received them, his forehead girded by its wreath of human hair, the image of Makemake suspended from his back, his chest naked where the god stared out with huge, wide-open eyes. Who would not have been awed by him?

He ordered the warriors to hoist the Living Faces they had toppled in feuds. If Vaitéa's woodlands were restored someday, Miru told them, those statues could be moved to their sites on rails hewn from the wood of new trees. In the meantime more giants of stone would not be chiseled from the quarry. There were more urgent tasks.

The manbird also invited seers and sorcerers to the house at Rano Raraku, healers, diviners and lords of the clans. All went but Marama, who still rankled in her cave, and Neira, who continued lamenting her losses. To each person Miru explained the sources of their island's decay, the need to renew fields and forests, the sea and fishing grounds. He was aware that many would not understand: their livelihoods depended on the earth and ocean. The manbird required their patience and their help.

He decided to address the whole people by calling them to the cliffs at Orongo. A multitude assembled on the ceremonial grounds, where King Hiti, warlords, priests and nobles waited. With the god tied to his body, resplendent in the manbird's wreath, escorted by his family and loyal soldiers, Miru strode through the crowd. As he walked among them, the islanders looked at him in wonder.

He mounted the platform on the palisade jutting over the sea. Knowing that dissent was more unlikely from a seated crowd, Miru asked for all to kneel or sit. He surveyed the tribes. Women, children and men with drawn faces and emaciated bodies gaped at him.

"Raas and Tuus, my people," he started, "listen! These are the truths we must live by." Wishing he could speak with Marama's old music of words, Miru lifted the eggshell. "Vaitéa is broken," he said in a resonant voice, "like the tern's egg in my hand. If we don't heal and care for it, our island will die. We will die too." Onlookers murmured while the surf roiled below.

"Our first king made a prediction," Miru recounted. "He told our people that we would flourish as long as we loved the earth and sea. We ignored his prophecy—we stopped being friends to the world." Looking inland, Miru said, "We leveled our forests." He turned to the ocean, saying, "We depleted our shores." Before facing the tribesmen again, he paused. "We don't have enough trees to build boats, firewood to cook and heat our houses. Fish and shellfish are vanishing from our coasts. Birds have died out or fled Vaitéa." Once more the manbird stopped to let the listeners absorb his words. "We're unable to nourish our own children. The time has come to rescue them, our island and ourselves. Every valley, every mountain, every tree and flower, each wave and inlet, each bird, each fish, everything alive must be cherished and protected."

Miru lowered the eggshell. When wind gusted from the ocean, he thought of Kenetéa. He drew a slow breath. "My people, hear me! From now on all woods, groves and fields will be guarded by soldiers from the clans." The manbird fixed his eyes on Nuku, who sat by his father, glowering. "The felling of trees will be punished sternly." Many of the warlords mumbled.

"In place of timber we'll burn grass," Miru declared, "plantain tops and strips of sugarcane. These won't heat our houses as well as wood—we'll be cold in the winter. And for a long time our food will be seasoned by hunger." His last word echoed against the fire-rocks. "Until the scorched fields are planted and harvested, until our forests thrive again, until fish, shellfish and birds multiply, we'll live on the sparse crops that have survived. We'll know days of want. These truths apply to all, from workers and soldiers to myself and the king." Plump Hiti frowned. "Transgressors won't be spared," Miru added.

He contemplated the people. As if to embrace them all, he opened his arms. "*Ma Makemake, ma Tangaroa,*" he chanted. Silently he invoked the graceful spirits of Ragi too. "I ask for your aid," he told the crowd. "Together we may have the strength to save our island."

Most of the listeners were uneasy. Those women and men, who had already endured unbearable hardships, were being enjoined to further deprivations. Yet others were willing. Never had a king, priest or manbird entreated them with such honesty, compassion and knowledge of their sea-battered home.

Some Tuu warlords were relieved to follow an Ariki from their own clan. Others dreaded Miru's impartial judgments more than they feared their enemies. They were suspicious of a man who ignored the blood-strife.

A few Raa leaders observed the new measures. They felt bound by their oaths, compelled by the manbird's aura. But most could not forget the rivalry. They began to ignore the pledge they had made on the day of his victory. How could a Tuu boy—with sixteen summers and freckles on his cheeks—how could he claim their allegiance?

Renga Roiti asked to be the manbird's messenger. Back and forth she traveled to report on the young trees. It did not take long before she brought dismal news. With tears pouring from her eyes, she told Miru that warriors from both tribes had chopped more saplings and were using the supple limbs for weapons.

"And there's something else," Renghi said, looking almost ashamed. "Families in both tribes are cutting trees and clearing land in order to sow crops and escape starvation. Others are burning lumber to enrich the soil."

The Ariki ruminated. "I understand those people, sister. I've failed to write the new laws in their hearts." At that moment Miru believed his cause was futile. But he did not reveal his despair to Renga Roiti, whose hope sustained him.

Kuihi and Kuaha also served the manbird. Although the dwarves had aged, they could still move with stealth. Miru charged them to keep the warlords under surveillance. The twins learned that Hiti and Nuku were chafing at the reforms, sending out spies and plotting against Miru and his allies. They discovered that shark-faced Engo had rejected the changes too; he roamed at night, stalking his foes, tempting Koro's son to intervene.

"Resist or die"—Ihu's and Marama's warning stuck in the manbird's head. Miru had reached the point of action. He moved swiftly.

First he asked Renga Roiti to speak with the sorceress. With her uncle she traveled to Kote Pora. Ihu stayed at the cavern's mouth while the young woman entered the sanctuary.

As soon as the priestess saw Renghi, she inquired, "What does Miru want from me?"

"A potion to make a man sleep."

"What kind of man?"

"A mountain of a man." The woman grimaced. "Marama," keen-witted Renga Roiti said, "my brother's close to fulfilling your prophecies." She knew how to turn the seer's vanity to account.

Marama breathed heavily. On tiptoes Renghi waited for her response. "I may decide to help," the cagey witch offered, receding into the cave's heart.

Ia's daughter listened to the surf as she waited. Carrying a small gourd sealed by a plug of tapa, Marama returned. Renga Roiti tucked it beneath her waistcloth.

Meanwhile Miru had sent both dwarves to the harbor. There they found the two old mariners and ordered them to rig *Mahina-i-te-pua* for launching. Next the manbird invited Prince Kaimokoi, who owed Miru his life, to visit the sun-bleached house. He directed that soldier to be ready if needed. When the king's son had gone, Miru called Engo, chief warlord of the Tuus, and told him the same.

He summoned Nuku to the house on the volcano's slope. Seated in the manbird's chair—sculpted with images of eggs and sooty terns—Miru waited for the soldier's arrival. Renga Roiti crouched a few steps away, trembling. Two armed sentries flanked the door.

When Nuku crossed the threshold, the space looked suddenly smaller. He shivered from the cold in a room where no firewood warmed the hearth; he must have recalled his dank grotto on Motu Nui. The burns on his thighs were seeping pus.

"Sit," the Ariki told him. Nuku squatted on the floor of tamped earth.

Renghi stood and moved close to her brother. The king's older son appalled her more than death or hunger. Wind gusted through the entrance.

"Nuku," the manbird said, "I asked the warlords to honor their oaths and respect the truths of Orongo. You haven't complied."

"Do you expect me to sit back while Engo flouts the truce?" The force of the prince's voice made the eggshell sway on the roof-beam. "He goes on killing my soldiers as he did before."

Miru inhaled twice before responding. "I'll deal with Engo myself. I've called you here because my spotters have seen you and your men slashing trees." He paused to stifle his outrage. "You deserve to be punished for your crime, Nuku." The tone of Miru's voice reminded Renghi of their father's, raising the light down on her arms.

"Will you punish Shark-Face too?" the prince asked.

"I'll treat Engo and all offenders alike."

Nuku's belly growled. It was time that the warlords felt the famine preying on the people, Miru thought. He and his sister exchanged glances.

"See my stomach?" he asked the king's son, touching his wounded belly. Nuku did not deign to look at the knife-gash he had made on his rival's abdomen. The weapon he had wielded now lay in a heap of ashes.

"No—you look at my legs!" the warrior shouted, lurching to his feet. The guards closed around him. "I said look!" the prince screamed as if those soldiers were not pointing their spears at his chest and stomach. He showed his scalded thighs, thick as tree trunks.

Miru signaled the sentries to lower their weapons. He set his eyes on the warlord. "You breached taboo by attacking me in the cave, Nuku. I defended myself. The king's order was to hurl an offender from the cliffs." Miru allowed his words to settle in the soldier's mind. "You also lied when you claimed to have found the tern's egg." Nuku averted his eyes, and the Ariki paused once more. "But I can't forget that you rescued me on the shore of Motu Nui. For that reason I'm going to offer you a reprieve."

The corners of the prince's mouth curved upward. "Will you pardon Engo?"

Miru did not reply. Instead he stated, "You could have tried to drown me on the swim back to our island. Why did you not do it?"

Nuku looked at the manbird: "I'll confess that I considered it. But you aren't the only one who has virtue—I couldn't drown a man who saved my brother from the sea."

Yet you almost killed me in the cave, Miru told the warrior in silence, and you're conspiring against me.

Nuku looked at Miru with his eyes the color of oyster shells: "I also knew that we could defeat your tribe even if I'm not the manbird."

Miru paused for the last time. "Renga Roiti," he called. "Please serve the king's son."

She handed Nuku a wooden bowl of Marama's libation. He drank. Sleep fell over him like a fog.

Renghi rushed to find Engo. When Miru asked the warlord to carry his rival to the harbor, the orphan was glad to avail. He and two of the manbird's guards covered Nuku in a sheet of tapa cloth and lugged him to the beach, where the double canoe rested on the sand, its bows pointing seaward. As soon as the soldiers had left, the mariners dragged Hiti's son to the hold. They shackled his hands and feet with cords of braided hibiscus.

Brother and sister waited for Engo's return. When he appeared, they thanked him for his help. How could the shark-faced soldier have guessed that a manbird from his own tribe would dispatch him also?

"Renga Roiti," Miru said, "please serve the warlord."

Engo gulped the potion, and sleep descended on his eyes. Renghi raced to find Kaimokoi, who obeyed instructions by hauling the warrior's body to the ship, aided by Miru's guards. The sailors heaved Engo into the hold and fettered him at Nuku's side.

With a third mariner to complete the crew, the longboat slipped away in the dark. When Nuku and Engo wakened from the vessel's tossing, the seamen drugged them with a fresh dose of Marama's remedy; the warlords sank into a profound slumber. In two days the canoe landed on the crag of Motiro, the wind's home, where the swallows had homed on the inbound voyage from Ragi.

While a pair of the sailors lifted the groggy soldiers from the hold, one at a time, the third stayed at the helm. The two men towed the warlords up the stony beach. With their legs lashed by cords, Nuku and Engo howled, trying to untie themselves and kick the mariners, who boarded the boat again.

As wind caught the ship's sails, the seafarers looked back. Both warriors were flailing their arms, leaping up and down, cursing them from the shore.

Miru had sent the twins as lookouts to the harbor. When the canoe hove into sight, they scurried to the manbird's house with the news. "If those assassins refuse to make peace," he told the dwarves, standing by his sister, "they can fight each other on that barren rock with Renga Roiti's birds for company."

He ordered sentries to stand watch over the twin-hulled craft. That seasoned vessel had one more trip to make.

194

King Hiti bawled for Nuku's exile and dishonor. Wicked tongues said the true reason for the chief's misery was the stark diet imposed by Miru. Hiti's mountain of a belly dwindled, and the royal raiment engulfed him.

Without his son to sustain his throne, the king retreated to his palace, almost forgotten by the people. He pined for death. Soldiers, priests, nobles, servants and musicians abandoned the longhouse. Many followed Prince Kaimokoi in supporting the manbird. Miru had proven his worth and won the Raas' approval for the time being.

Those tribesmen banded together with Tuu warriors to defend the final stands of seedlings. Some also guarded newly planted fields of yams, sweet potatoes, taro and sugarcane. But mutinous warlords often evaded the loyal troops, cutting saplings and stealing harvests. Meanwhile Hiro's tears did not fall. Many trees and crops withered.

Other soldiers helped the old mariners and fishermen to patrol the coast. Mussels, oysters, clams, eels and lobsters began to replenish slowly. But rebel warriors defied the laws, hunting for shellfish at night on the farthest shores.

Soon enough King Hiti joined his ancestors. A small number of Raas bemoaned his death. With the elder prince banished, Kaimokoi had become heir to the throne.

After rituals of mourning he traveled to the volcano. Kaimokoi's escort remained beyond the stone barrier while their lord entered the whitewashed house, where Renga Roiti was visiting her brother. The prince was taken aback when he saw the young woman at Miru's side.

"May your father's soul spin free of his body," the manbird told Kaimokoi.

"May he join his ancestors beyond the sun's gates," Renghi added. The prince held his eyes on Miru's sister, who blushed and withdrew to a dark corner of the room.

Kaimokoi looked aged and fatigued. "You've stopped most of the killing, Ariki," he said, "and brought us a small flame of hope. And you've passed your seventeenth summer." For the first time Miru remembered that he was a year older. "I've come to offer you the kingship," Kaimokoi ended.

Neither sad nor happy, Miru smiled. He would have liked to embrace Kaimokoi. But the manbird recognized who he was now, who his friend had become. From the shadows Renga Roiti watched.

"In three months," Miru replied, "the year of Calm Water will close. Until then we should pray for a new king, Kaimokoi, and for rain to nourish our trees and crops. You and your men must continue defending the truce."

"Thirst for revenge still burns in the warlords' throats. Some of those men are ruthless."

Miru looked deeply into the man's eyes. "Those who violate the truths of Orongo will be punished like your brother and Engo."

"Why don't you kill the offenders?"

"Because I want to break the circle of death." Old Te Rahai's injunction resounded in Miru's ears. "Vengeance does not bring freedom, Kaimokoi. It turns on the avenger, eating out his heart." He paused. "I want you to shun force except in the direst need. If you're compelled, use it with restraint. If you must join battle, do it gravely, like a man attending a funeral."

The prince looked at Miru as if he were seeing him for the first time. In a moment he said, "I'll do whatever I can to help, Ariki."

Kaimokoi departed. Renga Roiti approached her brother and hugged him tightly. "I'm proud of you for following our grandfather's desire," she said. "You'd be a good king."

Miru smiled. "I think Kaimokoi's fond of you. Did you see how he stared?"

Renga Roiti did not answer her brother's question. She merely stated, "Remember what you told me the last time."

The younger prince was staunch as the toromiro trees incised on his body. He led Raa and Tuu warriors against the men who spurned the new laws. Kaimokoi and his troops scouted woods, fields and coasts. Shoulder to shoulder they fought to keep the insurgents at bay. Resistance was keen. The allies suffered losses and reversals. Like the eggshell that hung in the stone house, the truce was tenuous: it hung in the air like a feather, prey to every gust of wind.

Gradually the peace began to hold. It was then that the meaning of *Vai Riva* dawned in people's minds. All but the oldest islanders had never lived without fear, without danger abroad at night. Miru had brought them a respite and a chance for a different life. More men joined him to oppose rebellion.

In the final months of isolation Miru found strength. He purged his rancor, aware that he was Tangaroa's son and Makemake's anointed, a manbird for both tribes. Recollecting his grandfather and the graceful spirits of Ragi, he strove to have a quiet heart. In dreams, meditation and prayers he came to accept his father's death; in some ways Koro seemed closer than when he was alive and away at war. Miru also resigned himself to Kenetéa's absence. It was a cost of the voyage, for the growing seeds and shoots, for serving Vaitéa's people. He stopped living as a slave of his heart and learned to be alone again.

One morning Renga Roiti appeared at the whitewashed house. Miru was always elated to see her, the only person to whom he could reveal his inmost life. They rubbed noses and embraced.

"Renghi, I must to tell you something."

"What?" The eager look on her face reminded Miru of the little girl she had been.

"I felt our father's presence after the manbird contest."

"At Orongo?"

"Yes."

"So did I, Ru."

He did not look surprised. "Remember what our mother told me when he fled from our house?"

"That you must reconcile with our father someday."

"Yes. I've made peace with his memory."

"So have I."

"What do you mean?"

"Do you think you're the only one whose father disapproved of our mission, who stormed from the great-house and did not return?" Renghi's eyes brimmed with tears. "The only one whose father was killed and disgraced by Raas, who couldn't say goodbye to his wife and children, who never had a funeral? Have you forgotten that Koro had a daughter too?"

He would never think of Renga Roiti as a younger sister again. As much as Miru was a man, she was a woman. For her part she loved him dearly. Whenever the manbird's duties allowed, she visited her brother in the sun-drenched house.

The period of *Vai Riva* ended without rain. In spite of the drought Miru felt relief and a lightening of his heart when he removed the wreath of women's hair and the figure of the god from his back. He wrapped Koro's straw-colored cape around his shoulders. He lowered the cracked egg from the roof-beam and held it in one hand, regarding the sunlight that shone through its shell. In the year of Miru's term it had bleached to a chalky white. "It's dry and brittle like our island," he said to himself, to the spirits or the air.

He hiked across the volcano's flank, down a trail leading to the white gannets' roost. The colony of birds, smaller than before, clustered on a ridge above the sea. Extending their wings, males performed their courtship dance in front of hens, making a long, fervid cry that brought a distant afternoon reeling back to Miru's mind.

He walked through the birds and onto the ledge. Facing the islet of Motu Nui, where he and the prince had swum, he cast the tern's egg. It flew from his hand, hovered over the waves and alighted softly on the surface. Miru watched it dance on the sea's foam. The eggshell filled with water, rolled, then sank into the surf. He was almost free again.

Chapter 14

Halo of Royalty

He **climbed** windswept Terevaka. On the peak Miru discovered an aged, withered great-palm. For the first time in months the clouds opened, and Hiro's tears poured on the island. The rain and the tree helped him reach a decision.

He dug out the palm's dead trunk. In the rain he tugged it back to the royal sanctuary, where he rooted it at the center of the courtyard. He lopped the branches, pruned the gnarled trunk, shaping it deftly with an obsidian adze. He trued it to the line for a bedpost. Around the tree Miru built a room of close-set stone. He roofed the chamber with thatch of reeds and sugarcane. It would become the home of his heart at Anakena.

Kaimokoi ordered the palace to be purified with smoke, aired, cleaned and painted with shell-lime. In a sober rite the prince ceded the kingship.

The Ariki knew his mind. "The first thing I want," he informed the household, "is to tear down the taboo stones around the residence. I'll divulge the second shortly."

Palace guards razed the wall that separated the royal longhouse from the people. After spending time in contemplation, Miru left the sanctuary before dawn one day, when nobody would spot him. Again he was seeking the unattainable. As he strode on the familiar trail, he imagined a girl and boy walking beside him, laughing, playing in the grass. Her black hair blew in the wind.

The sun rose above the world's edge. Miru circled steep cliffs, now clear of fog, bathed in sunlight. He crossed the taboo grove. Without raising his spear, with wide-open eyes, a sentry watched the new king pass.

When Miru arrived at the cavern's mouth, the white virgins and their guardians flocked around him. They were dazzled by his bearing and the light. All dispersed in the woods.

Miru entered the cave. Allowing his eyes to adjust to the darkness, he moved cautiously. Before long he found Kenetéa seated in a chamber illuminated by a torch. She was grooming her hair; it fell in waves to the floor.

When she saw him, the young woman dropped her whaletooth comb, sprang to her feet and sped into a tunnel. Miru tried to follow. Soon he was bewildered in a maze of passages. With drooping shoulders he plodded from the cave.

Like the boy who had once mourned Kenetéa's exile, he wandered over meadows, shores and woodlands, searching for the spots where they had been together. Those places sharpened his longing. The days and their nights seemed endless. In his memory the girl dwelled like a plaintive ghost.

Although his thoughts were elsewhere, Miru began to serve as chief of the island. Some Raas revolted against the new ruler because their tribe had lost the kingship. Loyal soldiers, led by Kaimokoi, drove the rebels into remote parts of Vaitéa.

Meanwhile Miru felt as impatient as the boy whose totem spirit was the leaping dolphin. When he could bear it no longer, he returned to Ana o Keke. Like a shadow in a dream, Kenetéa flew from him again.

Brooding, he walked to the borderlands. Miru did not dye his hair or change his clothes: only a few warriors patrolled the line, allies who maintained the truce. He ascended the round hill and walked into the valley. There was no need for him to scan the precinct: the house's master was dead.

"I forgive you," Neira told him at her doorstep, reaching for Miru's hands. He could hear the grief in her voice. The widow paused before speaking again. "You were trapped in the circle of death. But now you're close to bringing peace to the tribes."

They conferred. She implored him to be patient and to honor Kenetéa's bereavement. Brushing Miru's hair and brow with her palms, Neira blessed him. He walked back to the longhouse, where he secluded himself to pray, ponder and wait.

Miru resumed his duties as king. Slow and heavy as stones the days and months passed.

When spring had given way to summer, when he could refrain no more, he ventured to the virgins' cave for the third time.

Holding her head high, Kenetéa walked into the last light of day. Miru's heart fluttered like a trapped bird. He was dismayed to see how she had changed: her skin looked paler than ashes, her cheeks were hollow, rings shaded the pools of her eyes. For all that he was struck by her dreadful beauty. It flowed not only from Kenetéa's comely face and figure but from a hidden place inside her, somehow spared the full havoc of her people and her family.

She turned to reenter the cave. Miru followed. Her white limbs melted into the shadows. Listening for the sound of Kenetéa's padding feet, he treaded behind her. Dankness rose around them.

She walked down narrow passages, farther into the earth. At the end, in the island's deepest core, Kenetéa halted. She and Miru could no longer hear waves beating on the cliffs. Silence enclosed them.

During those years the cavern had become her home, where her eyes could see in the gloom. Kenetéa looked at Miru. Did she perceive the former manbird's presence, the king's, the gods and goddesses inside him?

Unable to see her well, he listened to her breathing. "Why must we always meet in the dark?" Miru asked. He could hardly hear his own words; they sounded lost in clouds and mist, as if they had crossed endless distances.

"Because you've stolen the light from me." Kenetéa paused. "First you took Mohani. Next you killed my father before my mother's eyes. Then you banished—"

"Two men with bloody hands."

"Your hands are also stained with blood."

Miru had never heard such anger in Kenetéa's voice. He had sensed it in the words of people who visited the manbird's house, women and men from both tribes. But their rage had been his own. Now the young woman's fury pierced him like a lance. She's the daughter of Raunui, he told himself.

Miru paced toward Kenetéa. "Will you wash the blood from my hands?" His words ached with all the years of separation, with the fear that she would vanish again.

She did not reply. Nor did she walk away. Kenetéa's anguish, shared with Miru, held her there.

When he moved nearer, she recoiled. "Leave me alone with my pain. Do you think I'll love you because you're the king?"

"Come into the light with me."

Kenetéa did not reply. Her isolation at Ana o Keke had taught her the power of quiet. Miru had learned it too, on the sea, on the green island and in the manbird's house.

It was then they began to feel the dead approaching. There was old Te Rahai and Koro, Raunui and Mohani, more fallen warriors from the tribes, people who had died of famine and disease. Entwining their arms, they converged around Miru and Kenetéa, forming a circle, a thick web of souls crowding the pair together. Those shapes moaned, wailed and shrieked with voices that sounded like calls of distress from wild birds or animals. The damp air swelled with howls that reverberated through the cave's tunnels, a dirge spun out of calamities, time and desolation.

"We'll also wither away," Kenetéa murmured. "Like these shadows."

"Yes," Miru said.

With the ends of his fingers he skimmed her arm. He felt its slightness, the bones beneath Kenetéa's skin. She sensed a softness that was new in a man's touch. Gently she dropped her arm.

Miru grazed her wrist. She withdrew it from his reach. What could she find in me that would make her consent, he mused: a likeness to herself, an echo of her suffering, exile and loneliness?

Miru held out his hand. It touched Kenetéa's, whose fingertips seemed light as leaves. The two could feel one another's pulse-beats. As the host of dead people faded into the blackness, the young man and woman did not stir.

He peered at her. She did not look away. In spite of the cavern's murky light, Miru thought he discerned the seeds in the depths of her eyes, those drops of the moon. He saw into Kenetéa—her sorrow, her losses, her striving against the feud. In the cave's heart he recognized her, also himself, whom he had never known well.

Kenetéa watched carefully. Her eyes saw straight through him—his sacrifice, his heartache, the waters and soaring woods of Miru. She recognized him and herself, whom she had never known with such clarity. In the world above stars wheeled across the sky.

Kenetéa lifted Miru's killing hand. With the petals of her lips she brushed it. She lapped his palm, wetting it with warm saliva. She lowered his hand, took the other, raised it and licked the sea-worn skin. Kenetéa's tears and his own also moistened his palm.

A flush moved up Miru's wrist and arm. "Thank you," he said. Like a pair of youthful trees they stood facing each other.

"My mother visited," Kenetéa said, barely holding back more tears. "She told me how much you longed to see me here. She also said you're the last one who could save me and our island."

"Do you believe her?"

Kenetéa hesitated before responding. As she looked at the floor, she said, "I don't know. All I can tell you is that my knees turn to water when I'm near you. I used to hate myself for it and I feared you. Now I've come to accept it."

If Kenetéa had lifted her eyes, she would have seen the rapture on Miru's face. Instead she swung her head, as though she had freed herself of a weighty burden. Her hair swirled against his brow, his neck, shoulders and chest. Listening to each other's breath, they stood without speaking.

Miru inched closer to Kenetéa. He pressed his body against hers until there was no air between them. He embraced her, they rubbed noses and kissed, drinking the moisture from each other's tongue, teeth and mouth. As Kenetéa's frail body trembled in his arms, Miru felt dizzy and thought he would faint.

She caught her breath. "You've learned to cherish our island and our people," she told him. "I can see you truly now."

"I can see you also," he gasped.

"Ru."

"Téa."

They did not say more. In the dark and silence they knew each other beyond names and words. Moisture dripped from the cavern walls.

Neither Kenetéa nor Miru disclosed the events of that night. The white virgins and their guardians did not dare to think or speak the forbidden, the taboo, the unimaginable. The king retired from the cave and reached the royal sanctuary by moonlight.

At dawn he dressed in Koro's straw-colored cape. Miru led Kaimokoi, priests and nobles to the family home, where his mother, sister and uncle joined the procession. From there they traveled across the border to the great-house in the valley, where they invited Neira to follow.

The road was lined with men back from the wars, women and their children, the elderly. When Miru and the others passed, the onlookers lowered their heads. He winced, feeling a sudden pang in his chest, like the pinch of a crab's claws. He wanted to hold all those people in his arms.

At Ana o Keke, deep in their island's heart, the king received Kenetéa. The rituals have been lost in time. So the union of the tribes was born.

Crowds witnessed the stately homecoming. Arrayed in a sweeping red and yellow cape, her skin bleached whiter than milk, Kenetéa smiled at them, queenly and dignified. She and Miru walked arm in arm.

The two sneaked glances from the corners of their eyes; they were not used to seeing one another in daylight. The falling sun shone on their faces. Like tall trees their shadows trailed behind them.

Old people from the tribes, who recalled when Miru and Kenetéa had played together as children, saw the halo of royalty around them. Yet some still believed the new king was mad. Others said the same of his queen, the first to wed a chief from the other tribe. Do not all great men and women have a few birds in their head?

At dusk the procession arrived at Anakena. King and queen crossed the threshold of the palace, where Miru lit a torch. Eager as a boy he showed Kenetéa the room he had built for them around the palm tree. They reclined on the bed with its fragrance of freshly cut wood.

That night, followed by more nights and their days, they tried to make up for stolen months, the long seasons spent apart. Miru and Kenetéa reveled in the astonishment of being together without haste or peril, without guards crying watches, unbound in the light at last. Both felt life's passing sweetness.

They strolled on the pink sands of Anakena, where they swam in the green cove. As they walked on its beach, arm in arm, stepping through the foam, he said, "Téa, we're in the sea and on the land at the same time. They're different but also one."

"Ru," was all she said.

They roamed the woods, hills, fields and coasts. As they had done when they were children, they explored the recesses of their island. There they found themselves once more.

The stage of yearning was past. Miru and Kenetéa began to restore the childhood of their joy. Their happiness was marked by trials too—theirs, their families' and the people's. Now and then they missed the solitude that had been their friend. Their widowed mothers remained disconsolate. One or two stubborn warlords stirred troubles.

Yet most days took on a brilliance of light and the sea. The king and queen rescued parts of their lives that had been broken in the past, deepened by years, pain and knowledge. He was with her, she gave herself to him, and the sun yielded to stars rolling across the sky. As each came to know the other well, their love grew. Their hearts were full.

Rain fell, crops rooted, forests revived. Swiftly as breaths of wind the seasons whirled past. Miru fathered a son by Kenetéa. Months flowed like a rushing stream, and she gave birth to a daughter.

In their bed of palm wood the couple curved their bodies around the children. Kenetéa and Miru had saved two dying families and formed a new one. It would endure for a long time.

The Ariki was a firm chief. He brooked no infringement of the truce. The last rebels failed to shatter Vaitéa's calm. He shipped them to the barren rock, where they kept company with Nuku, Engo and the birds.

Perhaps the former prince finally learned to build a fire on that bald crag, the wind's home.

For now the days of pillage and bloodshed had ended. Waters of peace covered the island. The young king taught both tribes what he had only imagined on the road to the sacred mountain: love could be as strong as fear and hatred.

The people knew his kindness. He had broken the circle. That and restoring Vaitéa's woods—not winning the sacred egg or earning the kingship—were Miru's greatest feats.

Although he was a wise ruler, he could still be as impulsive as a leaping dolphin. When his totem brothers approached the shore, sometimes Miru swam, dove and played with them. In the fall he shocked the islanders by leaving home to ride the big break, the high surf that strikes Vaitéa once a year. On the pebbled beach at dusk, when the wave-sliders brought in their reed mats, when crowds flocked around bonfires, while the ocean heaved beyond them, Miru enthralled his people with poems, songs and stories. As he recited them in the growing dark, he wiggled his toes on the sand, smiling.

Meanwhile red-haired Renga Roiti trained for the rites at Orongo. In the third year of her brother's reign she won the contest. When she climbed the cliffs and placed the tern's egg in Miru's outstretched hand, the little girl's smile shone on Renghi's face.

As the crowd cheered around them, as singers chanted hymns, she spoke softly in her brother's ear. "Ru, remember when the terns splattered your head?" The king could not suppress a smile of his own.

Renga Roiti had been the first woman of boats. Now she was the first to wear Makemake's image on her chest. Some shrank from applauding her victory; most respected it. After the ritual confinement she wedded Kaimokoi and bore children. The marriage secured bonds between the tribes.

Miru and Renga Roiti lived to see canoes built from heartwood of the spreading trees. They blessed new men and women of boats, those who had won the right to hold *Te Roku-o-witi*. Schools of fish on the sea bottom eyed the dark bellies of ships above them.

Brother and sister watched Ia and Ihu join their ancestors. Kenetéa's mother traveled beyond the sun's gates as well. The king and queen also witnessed the death of the last native coconuts, sandalwoods, palms and toromiros on their island. Relieving part of their sadness for the losses, stands of hibiscus—one of Kenetéa's totems—and mulberry—one of poor Mohani's—thrived along with the new tree. The people showed their ingenuity by employing its fruits for oil and food, burning its wood to cook and heat their homes, carving its limbs to make the rongorongo tablets that preserved their knowledge of the past.

In due time the soil bore rich harvests of yams, sweet potatoes, taro and sugarcane. Woodlands spread from one tip of Vaitéa to the other. Children saw treetops swaying in the breeze. Fires burned in hearths and warmed houses again. In streambeds fresh water flowed, nourished springs and filled empty wells. Birds of the air and sea thickened. On rocks and in tidepools shellfish increased. Tuna, whales and dolphins multiplied in the deep blue. The island resounded with laughter, feasting and songs.

The king announced that Tangaroa and Makemake could be worshiped together, as well as the goddesses who once roamed the island. Those graceful spirits came home to their retreats. After years of silence their music returned to Miru's mind, where it sang with Kenetéa's voice, with breezes rustling through trees and tides pulling on the shore.

Chapter 15

Deep into Time

Moon-faced **Marama** refused to pardon the king for disobeying her commands. She kept to herself at Kote Pora. When she knew the end was close, she relented and journeyed to the royal sanctuary. Miru and Kenetéa received her in the palace.

The priestess wore her old cape, whose color had yellowed with the years. She looked more ancient than the earth, wizened, shrunken and toothless. Yet her voice was clear when she finally spoke.

"Ariki and Kenetéa, I've prayed for your contentment and prosperity." The sorceress turned to the king. "Miru, I concede that you've fulfilled the prophecies and begun to heal our wounded island. But danger lies ahead of us. The moment has come to unveil the future." Marama observed the rulers with her good eye: the limpid, far-seeing eye of a girl in an aged woman's face. With the other she looked deep into time.

"Beyond the slippery path of death," she proclaimed, "there are people who are suspicious of the world. Their eyes are not the warm color of the earth, but cold and blue as the winter sea. Faster than a blink, they kill their enemies. One day the trade winds will blow them to our island. Those men will distrust what they find here—so they'll destroy it. And who will survive their coming? Like a storm of fire they'll sweep across Vaitéa! They'll try to steal our souls and cut the rope of wisdom. As much as the earth and sea you must protect it." In a corner of the longhouse a pair of flies droned.

Marama addressed the king. "Ariki," she whispered, "for the time being you've brought order to Vaitéa." A blush crossed the seer's weathered face. She raised her voice: "Yet it shall not survive the destruction." Marama paused to prepare the king and queen for her final prophecy. "The strangers will also drive away the spirits of the wind, the shadowy forests and the sea." Listening to those words, Miru and Kenetéa shuddered.

Marama looked up at the ceiling of thatched reeds and sugarcane. Rolling her far-seeing eye, she opened her lips and showed the dark crater of her mouth. She sang a dirge whose lines would echo in the royal consorts' memory:

O my mother,
O my father,
O my people.
Prepare yourselves
for the time
that is coming!

In a few days Marama died. With her staff tied to her shriveled hands, wrapped in her cloak, Miru buried the priestess in her secluded grove. He, Kenetéa and the tribes mourned. The moon concealed her face in sorrow.

For many summers Miru and his wife ruled. Their sway was wide as the wind, as the flight of sooty terns, as the sea around them. They had the calm of a man and a woman who are at home with themselves. They knew their own hearts.

At the end of his days death grew inside of Miru; he came to know it like a friend. He died in peace. Oh how Kenetéa felt her loss.

Men, women and children prayed that the king's soul would spin free of his body. They keened and wept, chanting:

Aûé, aûé,
what will become of us?
Miru, our Ariki!
Waves crash on rocks,
wind roars,
people cry for you.
Ariki, our king!
Aûé, aûé,
what will become of us?

His family washed Miru's corpse and rubbed it with oil. Some islanders wanted to adorn his body with fine clothing, with jewelry carved of whaletooth, conch and mother-of-pearl. Recalling her grandfather's words, Renga Roiti reminded them that men and women of boats sail lightly. So they dressed the dead king only in Koro's cape and a sash of tree bark.

In the slanting rain Miru's son and daughter and their children carried his body to the coast, where wind, earth and ocean meet. Surrounded by the people, they laid their lord in his canoe. *Mahina-i-te-pua* was a vessel for a king who had steered it across the sea.

They launched the death-boat to winds and tides. From the clouds Hiro's tears rained. The queen, her family and the tribes mourned for months and years.

Kenetéa ruled the island. She too was a guardian of Vaitéa, who had always urged Miru to remember the woods, fields and shores. Rongorongo singers praised their feats. Both passed into stories and songs.

Not long before the queen's death a strange object floated ashore. It was the trunk of a tree, rounded and smoothed, lashed to a crossbeam. Some people remembered three, others four sea-rusted nails driven deeply into the wood.

Questions and Topics
for Discussion

Wide as the Wind is a story written for all ages, so these questions and topics might be posed by teachers, members of book clubs or by individual readers who would like to reflect on the novel.

1. The story begins with young Miru stealing a yam from his family's kitchen, knowing this food has been cooked for his father. What does this episode tell us about the boy's character and the situation on Vaitéa?

2. Miru is both intrigued and repelled by the old sorceress Marama. How did you respond to this character?

3. Can you imagine a crisis in which you would have to leave your home, family and people to embark on a perilous journey like Miru's and Renga Roiti's? How might you deal with it?

4. In what ways does Renga Roiti break taboos and defy traditional roles assigned to girls and women on Vaitéa?

5. Kenetéa only appears directly a few times in the book, yet she motivates many of Miru's actions. Which of these do you think are most important?

6. The love story of Miru and Kenetéa might be compared to the tale of Romeo and Juliet. What are some similarities and differences between the novel and Shakespeare's tragedy?

7. How did you react to the sudden irruption of Kuihi and Kuaha into the novel? What do the twins add to the story?

8. Miru and Marama seem to engage in a constant duel of wits. At one point the narrator says, "The old priestess could not resist the temptation of pronouncing the last words." Do you think she does in fact have the "last word" in the novel, even though she dies before Miru?

9. What do you think the book's final image suggests: the trunk of a tree washed ashore, "lashed to a crossbeam," with "sea-rusted nails driven deeply into the wood"?

10. *Wide as the Wind* is based on the tragic history of Easter Island, one of the sites chosen by geographer Jared Diamond as an example of environmental disaster in his book *Collapse: How Societies Choose to Fail or Succeed.* Yet the author of the novel has called the island by an invented word, "Vaitéa," rather than its indigenous name, *Rapa Nui.* Why do you think he made this decision?

11. Can you draw any parallels between the collapse of Vaitéa/Easter Island and our current environmental situation?

12. The novel has been associated with a term now prevalent among ecologists and literary critics—"environmental imagination." Lawrence Buell, author of *The Environmental Imagination: Thoreau, Nature Writing, and the Formation of American Culture,* outlines what he believes "might be said to comprise an environmentally oriented work":

    i.   The nonhuman environment is present not merely as a framing device but as a presence that suggests human history is implicated in natural history;

    ii. The human interest is not understood to be the only legitimate interest;

    iii. Human accountability to the environment is part of the text's ethical orientation; and

    iv. Some sense of the environment as a process rather than as a constant is at least implicit in the text.

    How would you interpret "environmental imagination" in the context of *Wide as the Wind*? Does it match Buell's definition? Have you read any other books recently which you believe could serve as examples of this term?

About the Author

Edward Stanton's *Wide as the Wind* is based on ten years of travel and research on Easter Island, whose name he has changed in his novel in order to extend its imaginative reach to all of Polynesia. Born in Colorado and raised in California, he resides in Kentucky after having lived in Mexico, Argentina, Uruguay, Chile and Spain. Stanton is the author of eleven books, some of which have been translated and published in Spanish, Arabic and Chinese. *Road of Stars to Santiago*, the story of his 500-mile walk on the ancient pilgrimage route to Compostela, was called one of the two best books on the subject by *The New York Times*. Pulitzer Prize-winning writer James Michener said, "Edward Stanton recounts his adventures with stylish conviction." Stanton has also published fiction, poems, translations and essays in magazines, journals and newspapers in countries throughout the world. He has been a professor of literature at universities in the U.S., Europe and South America. The Fulbright Commission and the National Endowment for the Humanities have awarded him grants for travel, research and writing. His students and colleagues recently published a volume of essays in his honor. At present he is completing a travel memoir titled *VIDA: A Life*.